Saltwater Cove

ANJ Press

Pittsburgh

SALTWATER COVE
ANJ Press, First edition. November 2019.
Copyright © November 2019 Amelia Addler.
Written by Amelia Addler.

Cover design by Charmaine Ross at CharmaineRoss.com
Maps by Nate Taylor at IllustratorNate.com

For the love that makes us whole again

Introduction to *Saltwater Cove*

At 48 years-old, Margie Clifton never expected to be starting her life all over again. But when her brother gifts her a property on San Juan Island, that's exactly what she decides to do. After all, it's the perfect place to start a new business venture, provide a second home for her adult children, and recover from her nasty divorce. And if her new life happens to involve the town's gruff and ruggedly handsome Chief Deputy Sheriff? All the better.

The last thing Hank Kowalski wants is an emotional entanglement. It's only been two years since his beloved wife passed, and there's no way his daughter is ready to accept him dating anyone new. Still, there's something about Margie's quiet strength and beauty that draws him in, making him wonder if maybe a fresh start—and possibly a new love—is exactly what he needs in his life.

But Margie is harboring a secret—a dark one that threatens to destroy the new life she's worked so hard to build. Can Margie and Hank find the courage and faith to overcome all that stands between them? Or will their second chance at happily ever after be lost forever?

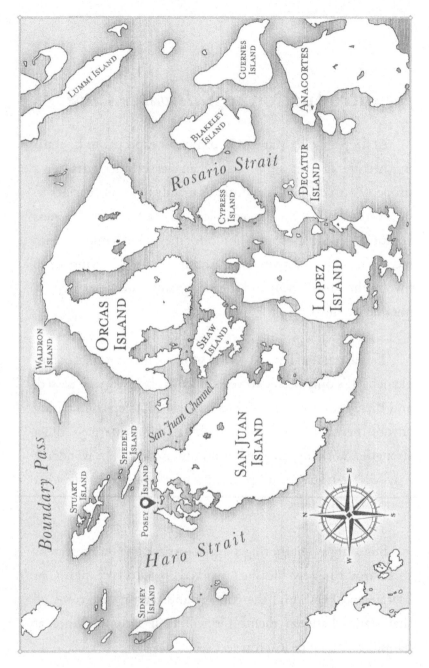

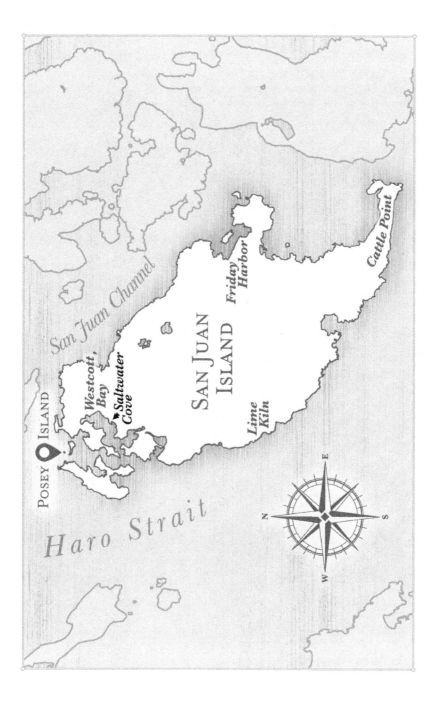

Chapter 1

The ferry hummed as it slowly made its way towards San Juan Island. Margie zipped her yellow rain jacket before slipping out of the warm galley and onto the ship's deck. The wind tore through her hair and chilled her face, but she didn't mind. She had the deck to herself and a beautiful view of Friday Harbor ahead.

She closed her eyes and took a deep breath. The air was certainly cleaner here than in Seattle. And the sweeping views of the islands were more stunning than what Puget Sound offered, as beautiful as it was. She liked living in the city, of course; it was where she built her life, and where her kids grew up. But her kids moved on and started their own lives, and she finally needed to move on, too.

"Margie? Margie Clifton, is that you?"

Margie took her eyes off of the glistening white sailboats in the distance. "Joan! Fancy seeing you here!"

Joan pulled her in for a hug. "Oh you know me and Ron, always looking for a romantic getaway. How are you? How're the kids?"

"Great, we're all great. And you?"

"Oh, we're all good too."

"Good." Margie paused – she really hadn't expected to see someone she knew, and she didn't want to babble too much.

"Are you just visiting for the weekend?"

And she *definitely* wasn't prepared to answer questions about what she was up to. "No, I uh – actually just bought a place on the island."

"Oh that's lovely! In town, or...?"

"No, on the west side." Ten acres, overlooking the water. But Joan didn't need to know that. It would sound like bragging, and Margie didn't like to brag. She was bursting with excitement, but the whole situation would be hard to explain.

"Oh that's right, your brother lives out here. He flies those little planes between the islands, right?"

"Yeah, that's right! You have a great memory." Technically, he *used* to fly planes between the islands. Now he was – well, that was none of Joan's business. And none of Margie's either, for that matter.

Margie cleared her throat. "Are you and Ron staying in town?"

"Yes, we'll be here for two days, then we're heading up to Orcas Island, and then back home. Just a quick little trip."

"That's lovely." Margie knew that if she kept talking, something would slip out that she shouldn't say, and then she wouldn't be able to stop herself. "Well, it was so nice seeing you, but I think we're getting close to the harbor, so I'd better get back to my car."

"Of course! Lovely seeing you too!"

Margie gave her a quick wave before rushing back inside and down the stairs to her car on the lowest level of the ferry.

She truly did enjoy chatting with Joan – she'd always liked her. Their eldest daughters were only one year apart in school so they always used to run into each other. Joan was a nice person.

"But that doesn't mean you should tell her your life story," Margie whispered to herself as she squeezed into the driver's seat of her Toyota. She promptly buckled her seat belt, then laughed at herself – she wouldn't be able to drive off of the ferry for at least ten more minutes. What did she think buckling her seat belt would do for her? Keep her safe in case every-thing turned into bumper cars down there?

She unbuckled herself and cracked the window. Just because Joan was a nice lady and their kids went to school together did *not* mean that Margie should tell her *anything* about the property she bought. That was the one thing that her brother Mike made her promise last month.

"If anyone asks where I am, say I'm working for an airline overseas," he said, handing her a blue ballpoint pen.

"Right, got it." She carefully signed and initialed her name where instructed. Mike explained that he was going back to work for the FBI again, but he couldn't tell her much. She knew not to ask questions. Her brother was nine years her senior, and though she was all of forty-eight years old, he could still make her feel like the baby of the family in situations like these.

"Congratulations," he said when they both finished sign-ing. "You just bought your first home."

She slipped him the $1 bill he'd requested in exchange for the property. "Are you sure I can't pay you something more reasonable?"

He shook his head. "This is all I'll need. Take care of it while I'm gone, okay?"

A voice boomed through the ferry's speaker system. "Drivers, please return to your vehicles and prepare to disembark."

Margie darted a hand into her purse, digging around for her keys. Why hadn't she had the *keys* ready instead of the seat belt! Finally she found them, trapped under a water bottle. She turned the key in the ignition and waited until it was her turn to drive off of the ferry and onto San Juan Island.

Slowly making her way off of the ship and onto Front Street, she felt a little nervous – she wanted to drop some things off at her new house before coming back into town, but the ferry was a bit late, so she was worried that she might run out of time.

She managed to get through town quickly, though, and made her way to the other side of the island. She wasn't technically taking the "scenic" route, yet it was still gorgeous. There was a quiet peace as she rode past the farms and little houses. Margie rolled her windows down, taking in the cool evening air.

When she reached the beginning of her new property, she had to get out of her car to unlock the chain that blocked the long driveway. She drove up, slowly, as rocks pinged the underside of her car and dust floated into her open windows. It didn't bother her in the least, and soon, she reached the top of the small hill which provided a breathtaking view of Westcott Bay.

It was even more striking than she remembered. The water shimmered delicately against the bright blue sky; puffy white clouds lazily drifted by, visible through the lush green trees on the borders of the property. Margie felt her heart starting to swell.

"There'll be time to stand around and gawk later," she said to herself. She pulled her car up to the house and quickly unloaded a few boxes. She was about to rush back outside when she saw an envelope taped to the back of the front door.

Hey little sis,

I'm really glad you took up my offer to buy this place. It's only halfway a dump, as you can see. I've been fixing it up over the last few months, but it still needs some work. I've left the names of some good contractors I know on the islands. Tell them you know me. Then, when that doesn't work, threaten them as you see fit.

I'm sorry I won't be able to be in touch for a while. I think you'll find that there's something magical about this place. If anything can help you put your family back together...this can.

- Mike

Margie swallowed, trying to break up the lump that formed in her throat. Her brother was not the sentimental type. He didn't share emotions or deal well, for example, with his little sister having a breakdown in front of him.

It was a few months prior that he had to witness it. Margie invited him for Christmas, and everything went horribly wrong. The one toilet in her apartment clogged, she burned the ham, and her downstairs neighbor came up *three* times to complain about how loud they were.

After all the kids turned in for the night, Margie lost it. Mike just stood there, arms crossed, as she cried.

"I'm sorry," she said, gathering empty plates and bits of wrapping paper. "I don't know what's gotten into me."

He stared at her before responding. "It's probably because you're trying to fit your three adult kids and your old brother into a one bedroom apartment for the holiday."

"Well, yes. That's it. That's all. Nothing a little plunger can't fix, right?" She only got to the sink before she started sobbing again. "I don't know, Mike. I don't know how to make it work. I feel like...days like this just make it seem like the divorce has ruined my family. Do you think I can ever make it right again?"

He thought for a moment. "I don't know."

Margie carefully folded the letter and tucked it into her pocket. She couldn't get sentimental right now; she was a woman on a mission.

Inside her purse, carefully zipped into a side pocket, was a photo of a woman. She reached in and pulled it out. There was no way she could put her family back together until she faced this woman from her past.

A woman whose secret was tied to her and her family.

A woman who was, apparently, dead.

Chapter 2

Hank leaned back in his chair, staring at the ceiling fan as it spun round and round. Twenty-eight minutes until his shift was over – barring any disaster, of course.

He heard the front door open, followed by some chatter between Lola, their secretary, and an unfamiliar voice. He kept watching the ceiling fan; it was just slightly more exciting than a clock.

"Excuse me, Chief? I've got someone who needs to talk to you."

"No you don't Lola," said Hank without looking away from the fan. "I'm sure that one of our fine deputies could help this person."

"Nope," said Lola matter-of-factly. "Everyone else is busy."

Hank looked around the room. It *did* look like everyone was on the phone or talking to someone. "They're all pretend-ing."

"I'll be right back," Lola said with a flat tone.

Hank put his feet back up on his desk and leaned back, closing his eyes. If this was someone coming to tell him that their neighbor's cat kept pooping in their garden, or that tourists weren't stopping fully at a stop sign, or that they suspected someone was harboring illegal fireworks – well, there was no need to open his eyes.

He heard Lola clear her throat. "This is the Chief Deputy Sheriff. Chief Hank, I'd like you to meet Margie Clifton. She's got some questions for you."

"Margie," he said, keeping his eyes closed as though he were meditating, "what's your emergency?"

"Oh! It's not really an emergency – I didn't realize that coming here would make it seem that way. It's actually – well it's something that's already happened, I don't think...well, I'm not sure actually..."

Hank opened his eyes. He didn't recognize the woman. Her yellow jacket was hard to look at, almost like looking into the sun. Or maybe it was all this nervous energy that she carried with her.

"Something that already happened?" he said slowly.

"I'm not sure. I just moved to the island – today, in fact. But last month, I was leaving the island after a visit and on the ferry I found this picture." She shot a hand into her large purse, pulling out a cut out from a newspaper. "And it just says 'In Memoriam.' But I know this woman, well, I knew her years ago. I just can't remember her name."

Hank leaned forward to look at the picture. "So you know her, but not her name?"

"Yes, I met her about...it must have been twenty some years ago. But then she disappeared from my life, and I could never find her again."

What kind of a tale was this lady turning? "And now you need to know her name?"

"Yes."

Hank sighed. There were posters up all over town for this dead woman. "Her name was Kelly Allen. She was killed in a hit and run a few months ago while visiting the island."

"Oh." Margie studied the picture closely for a moment before returning it back into her purse.

"Anything else?"

"One more thing. Kelly had a child. Would you happen to know his or her name?"

Hank sat up. "Listen lady. This is the sheriff's office. We're not here to investigate relatives of dead tourists. Maybe you should try a family tree website. Or Facebook."

The woman looked down, then back at him. "Oh, right. Well, thank you for your help, Chief...?"

"Hank."

"Chief Hank," she said with a smile.

He shook his head. "No, just Hank. That's – Hank's fine."

"It was nice meeting you Hank."

"Take care," he called out, leaning back in his chair and crossing his arms behind his head.

She seemed to take the hint and left without another word.

"Hey Chief," yelled one of the deputies, "I didn't know we were running such a tight ship around here and we couldn't help people find the relatives of lost friends."

"Didn't you know?" added another. "We don't have time to talk to island newbies with all this serious crime busting we're doing. Chief caught *two* dogs at large last week."

The room erupted into laughter.

"Any one of you boneheads could've stepped in to be her personal background checker," Hank replied. "But you were all pretending to be busy."

More laughter.

Hank sighed and looked at the clock. Eighteen more minutes. How was that possible? The week was really dragging. Plus he had to work the entirety of the upcoming Memorial Day weekend. That was always a doozy.

He leaned forward and unlocked his computer screen, figuring that he should check for any emails before he left for the day. When it finally loaded, he saw that there was nothing. Well that was good – he hated answering emails.

Sixteen minutes.

He opened up the program for background checks and searched Kelly Allen. Originally from Oregon. One husband, alive. One kid alive. Morgan Allen, twenty-two years old.

None of them had any criminal history. No aliases, no arrests. Nothing interesting. What did old sunshine jacket want with them anyway? Was she just another hoity toity rich lady looking for a cause? He wasn't going to let her bother this mourning family. They didn't need to deal with some bored socialite.

Hank managed to run out the clock on his shift by cleaning up his desk and washing out two coffee mugs that he'd allowed to sit for too long. He wished everyone a good night before heading out to his car; he decided to go to his favorite pizza place for dinner again. He knew that eating out often was bad for him, and he definitely put on some extra weight around the middle, but he couldn't bring himself to cook just for one person.

He got his usual two slices of pizza, washed them down with a Coke, and headed home. His house was dark and quiet when he arrived. He turned on the TV, folded some laundry, then got ready for bed. Four more days of work until he had a day off.

The next morning, he overslept his alarm and was fifteen minutes late getting to work. He used to hate being late – it really stressed him out. But now? Now it was just another entry on the long list of things that didn't matter.

When he opened the door to the office there was already a buzz of activity. It didn't take him long to see what the fuss was about – little miss sunshine was back at it again. He paused for a moment and studied her as she laughed and talked with the deputies. She was an older woman, certainly not bad looking. Was she flirting with the staff? And were they flirting *back?*

"Morning Chief," said Deputy Ball.

"What's going on?" asked Hank. He crossed his arms and stared at the group of deputies gathered around Margie.

She turned to him and smiled warmly. "There you are Chief! I was worried you were going to miss out."

Hank frowned. Miss out on what? One of the deputies stepped aside and he saw what she was talking about. Blueberry muffins, banana bread, and something else that he couldn't identify – but it looked amazing.

Ah. So she wasn't flirting. She was manipulating them – with baked goods.

"Is this your doing?" he asked.

She nodded. "It is! I love baking and I thought I would swing by and bring some treats this morning."

Hm. Not only did it look good, but now the smell hit him, too. The blueberries were overpowering. It'd been...well, a long time since Hank had homemade muffins. But just because this lady could bake didn't mean that she could use the sheriff's department to satisfy her whims.

"That's very nice of you," he said. "Is there anything that we can do for you today?"

Margie shook her head. "No! Not today. I will be applying for some permits soon. But I'm not even sure where to start."

"What kind of permits?" asked Deputy Ball, his mouth full of banana bread.

"Well, I'm trying to finish a renovation that my brother started. Mike Grady, do you know him?"

"Of course," replied the deputy. "Everyone knows Mike. He's helped us more than once – he'd always offer to look for lost kayakers or hikers from the sky."

Margie laughed. "Of course he never told me that he did that. He wasn't one to brag."

"No," Hank interjected. "He wasn't. Are you staying with him?"

"Not exactly..." she said. "He took a new job overseas – and he sold his property. To me. He thought that I could turn the barn into an event space. Like for weddings and things."

"Really?" said Hank. "Over on Westcott Bay?"

Margie nodded. "That's the place! And he had a lot of the renovation underway, but there are still a number of things I have to do before it's ready for prime time. And unfortunately, I'm much better at baking than I am at electrical work. Or plumbing!"

The group of deputies surrounding her rippled with laughter.

Hank uncrossed his arms. Maybe he wasn't entirely right about Margie. Mike was a great guy – he lived on the island for a while. Maybe it was even ten years. He flew small aircraft and helicopters. They even used to go fishing together sometimes on Hank's boat. If he'd have known that Margie was Mike's sister, he would have showed her a *little* bit of a warmer welcome.

"Well Margie, I'd be happy to help you with that myself. I've known Mike for years and, uh, I wish you would have mentioned that he was your –"

Margie waved a hand. "Oh I should have known that dropping Mike's name would help me around here. He did tell me to use his name to threaten contractors."

More laughter. Even Hank chuckled.

"Yeah, well, I can see that too."

"Anyway! My daughter is coming in from Anacortes on the ferry today, so I need to run a few more errands before I'm ready for her."

"Here, I'll see you out," said Hank. He opened the door and waited for her to pass through. He chose to ignore the snickers and "oohs" from the gaggle of deputies.

Margie's car was parked just outside the building.

"Well, thanks again for all the sweets," he said. "I can tell it's already lifting the mood of the staff for this weekend."

"Oh? Is it usually busy for you guys?"

Hank shrugged. "Sort of? We just get so many more people on the island that there's bound to be some trouble. Nothing serious of course – don't worry about that. But you know, noise complaints. Fireworks. Stolen garden gnomes."

Margie let out a high pitched laugh which caused even Hank to crack a smile. She had a nice laugh.

"That sounds very exciting," said Margie as she opened her car door. "I'll try to keep out of trouble."

"Please do! Or the deputies might set your bail as a cake!"

She laughed again.

What a *stupid* joke that was.

But she still laughed.

"Have a nice day!" she yelled before reversing her car.

Hank watched as she pulled out of the parking spot and drove away. Wait – why hadn't he told her the name of the daughter? He needed to make up for his cold meeting the day before.

Maybe he'd have some time this weekend to stop by and tell her about Kelly Allen. It was sort of a weird request, but now that he knew Margie wasn't some nosy socialite, it wasn't a big deal. What harm could it be to tell Mike's sunshine little sister the name of a dead woman's kid?

Chapter 3

"Honey! We have to go or we're going to miss the ferry!"

She heard a grunt from upstairs. Jade looked at her watch – she'd given him warnings at thirty, fifteen, and five minutes before they had to leave. She wasn't sure what else she could have done.

Her husband finally came downstairs. He was barefoot.

"I don't know why I have to go," he said, arms crossed.

"*Because*, my mom just moved onto the island yesterday. And I'd like to see her and see if we can help with anything."

"And?" He sighed. "I have an event tomorrow. We need to catch the evening ferry and sleep at home tonight so I can get ready like normal in the morning."

Jade went to the closet to fetch his shoes. "Don't worry, I promise that we'll make the ferry so we're back in our regular bed tonight. Come on, it'll be nice to go to San Juan. We always say that we're going to go, but it seems like we never make it. And it's such a short ferry ride away!"

"I'm sure we'll be going all the time now," Brandon said as he accepted the shoes. "So your wish came true."

"Okay, are you ready?"

"I guess."

Jade decided that it would be best if they took her car, because Brandon's car was a bit messy and he kept a lot of his

DJ equipment in the back. She wouldn't want it to get stolen when they left the car in the ferry parking area. Then he would be *really* upset that she made him go to San Juan for the day.

They parked and quickly got in line to board the ferry. They were just in time to walk on – if they were taking their car, they would have had to line up an hour before. Jade knew that wasn't going to happen, so she asked her mom if she minded picking them up at the ferry terminal.

It didn't take long to board and they made their way to the second floor. It seemed more crowded than usual, and Jade decided it must be because it was the Friday before Memorial Day, so people were headed to the islands for a bit of fun and relaxation. Jade wanted Brandon to have fun this weekend, too, but he hadn't said anything since they got on board.

"Do you want me to get you something from the snack bar? Nachos maybe? A beer?"

He shook his head. "No thanks. Don't you think your mom is going to make dinner?"

"I don't think so. I'd be surprised if her kitchen stuff is unpacked already."

"I mean, how much did she need to bring? Your uncle basically left all of his stuff there already."

Oh dear. This conversation was getting into dangerous territory.

"Oh, I don't know. Do you think we'll see any killer whales on the ferry ride?"

"It's too early in the season for that. And I bet he did leave everything," replied Brandon, looking out the window. "He sold her everything in that house: appliances, furniture –"

"To be fair," Jade interjected, "there's not a lot of furniture."

"Who cares? It's a huge house. It has four bedrooms and a finished basement. And that's not counting that barn."

"Yeah, it's a really nice house."

Brandon scoffed. "I can't believe your uncle just *gave* it to her. If he wanted to go and work halfway across the world, that's fine. But he could've let us live there. He didn't even have to *give* it to us! Although we could've put it to better use if he had."

Jade took a deep breath. It was better that he was saying this now than in front of her mother. She didn't know how to assuage him, but at least he was getting it out.

"I mean, that would've been nice, but we didn't have any right to it. He wanted it to go to my mom for some reason. I'm happy for her."

Brandon didn't respond. He just kept looking out the window.

Jade stood up. "So you don't want anything from the snack bar?"

He didn't answer, so she headed towards the snacks anyway. She didn't expect her mom to make dinner for them – she was probably just getting settled in. Jade decided on a soft pretzel and an iced tea for herself. She also got a pack of tuna and crackers for her husband, along with a Mountain Dew.

Those were two of his favorite things, it was sure to cheer him up.

She went back to the table where she'd left Brandon, but he was nowhere to be seen. She walked the length of the ferry looking for him, then wondered if maybe he went outside. She checked the front and the back of the ship with no luck. Finally, she went downstairs and found him sitting in a booth by himself staring at his phone.

"Hey I looked everywhere for you," she said, settling in across from him. "I got you a treat!"

"I couldn't stand all the kids upstairs. They were making so much noise."

"Oh, huh," Jade replied. She hadn't noticed. She took a bite of her soft pretzel. It was cold now, but when she dunked it in cheese, it was still pretty good. She sat for a moment, thinking of what she could say.

"You know, if we got serious about saving for a down payment, we could buy a house on San Juan Island. Or in Anacortes, or wherever you want."

"What's that supposed to mean? '*If* we get serious?'"

"You know, just like, make a budget. We both have to stick to it, but in a year or two we could have a real down payment."

He shook his head. "I don't know if I'm really ready for that right now. There's just a lot of moving parts with my business, and I don't want to hinder the growth because I have to worry about a budget."

"I mean, we could make it in a way so it's not going to hinder the business," she replied.

"Nah," he said, turning back to his phone. "Maybe in like a year or something."

Jade decided not to push it and instead focused on finishing her pretzel. When that was done, she leaned back in her seat and stared out of the window. She'd always loved taking the ferry between the islands. There was something so comforting about it – the enormous size of the ship made her feel safe and small. The low rumbling of the engines, the slow but steady movement slicing across the still waters – and always a chance to see killer whales, porpoises, or even humpback whales.

It was her absolute favorite way to travel – it was so comfortable, too! There was the onboard snack bar, bathrooms, and plenty of room to spread out and do puzzles or play games. When the weather was nice, she liked to stand on the outside of the ship and get a full view of the islands and water. It was a peaceful trip – never in a hurry, and they always got where they needed to go.

After about twenty minutes, she realized that Brandon wasn't going to snap out of his crabby mood anytime soon. She decided to head to the front of the ship and take in the sights.

Jade stood admiring the lush green landscapes and glistening water; she kept an eye out for whales and porpoises, but the water was still and flat. Sometimes, during quiet moments like this, she thought of the rivers of the underworld in Greek mythology. The ancient Greeks believed the afterlife was an actual place, and she could almost imagine that this ferry was quietly carrying her into the underworld.

Except it wasn't a horrible ride like on the river of fire (was that the River Styx? Or Phlegethon? She could never remember). What would the Greeks have called this, a ride that was heaven on earth? River SanJuanedos? Or maybe this was like the River Lethe – where virtuous souls slipped into oblivion, forgetting their earthly lives, as they were transported to paradise.

There was a buzz in her back pocket. Jade pulled out her cell phone – was Brandon looking for her?

No – it was a text from her mom. Jade smiled and opened it: a picture of the ferry coming into Friday Harbor. "I can see you already sweetie!!"

She laughed and took a picture of the harbor, sending it back to her mom. "I think I can see you too!"

Jade went back inside and found her husband. "Look, my mom is all ready to pick us up!"

He peered over and smiled. "That's cute."

"She said that she parked a few streets back so that we wouldn't get caught in traffic. Are you ready to go? I think we can get off soon."

"Yep, I'm ready. Let's go."

The tuna was still sitting on the table. She picked it up and put it into her purse – he probably would want it eventually. It didn't take long for the ferry to dock and they walked into Friday Harbor. Jade felt her spirits lifting as all of the other passengers slowly moved down the sidewalk with them.

There were young people, old people, families with kids and even dogs. Some people dragged suitcases behind them, while others traveled light like Jade and Brandon. The excitement from the crowd was contagious.

They crossed the street and Jade grabbed Brandon by the arm. "Let's take a picture! It's so cute here. I love all of these little shops and this view of the harbor."

"Okay," said Brandon. "Do you want me to take a picture of you?"

"No! Maybe we can ask someone, or take one of ourselves?"

"Let's just take one ourselves." He took her phone and outstretched his arm so that they both fit into the frame. He snapped two pictures. Jade tucked her phone back into her pocket and they continued up the hill towards the street where her mom was waiting for them.

Her mom spotted them and yelled out. "Jade, honey! Over here!"

Jade ran up and gave her a hug. "Hey Mom, thanks so much for picking us up. I can't believe you're here!"

"I can't believe it either!"

Brandon stepped forward and gave his mother-in-law a hug. "Margie, nice to see you."

"Did you guys need anything in town, or should we get going? I just pulled a lasagna out of the oven before I came to pick you up, so it should be ready when we get back."

Brandon smirked. "Jade ate on the ferry. She couldn't wait *one* hour."

"I didn't expect you to cook!" said Jade. "But don't worry, I always have room for your lasagna."

They piled into her mom's little car, Jade taking the front seat. "Mom, do you want me to reset your radio with the local stations?"

"That would be wonderful! I haven't had a chance to even think about that."

Jade busied herself with navigating and saving all of the best radio stations as she and her mom chatted back and forth about the move, packing, unpacking, and how easy it was to ship some of her belongings.

It was only a twenty minute ride to get from one side of the island to the other. That always surprised Jade – the island seemed so much bigger in her mind than it actually was, and before she knew it, they arrived at her mom's new house.

Jade had visited her uncle there before, of course, but this was different. She was so excited that she let out a squeal. "Mom! This is gorgeous!"

"I know! It's unbelievable. We'll do a tour later, but I don't want the lasagna to get cold."

They followed her through the front door. The table was already set with beautiful dishes and cloth napkins that complemented the color scheme of the room; Jade had never seen any of it before.

"Mom, when did you get all this stuff?"

She waved a hand. "Well, I just got so excited. I found the plates on sale and I decided to just go for it. Do you like them?"

"They're beautiful! And what about these napkins?" asked Jade as she spread a napkin across her lap.

"Oh, I made those myself. I saw the fabric and it seemed very San Juan Island to me."

Brandon cleared his throat. "They're very nice."

They cut into the lasagna and Jade served Brandon a large piece. "I don't think we've had Mom's lasagna in a long time – but it's to die for."

"Thanks so much Margie," he said.

Jade dug in. It was just as good as she remembered it. "So Mom, you said you're going to turn the barn into a place for weddings and stuff?"

"Yes," she said with a nod. "There's still a lot of work to be done, though."

"Oh it can't be that bad. I'm happy to come over and help. Have you thought about what you're going to name it yet?"

A smile broke across her mom's face. "I have, but I don't know if it's too...I don't know, I'm not sure if it works."

"What were you thinking?" asked Brandon.

She sighed. "Well, I kept trying to think of something with the word 'barn' in it. But then it just sounded like I was running a farm, and I'm not going to have any farm animals here. So then I was thinking...well, what about something like Saltwater Cove?"

"Oh my gosh," said Jade. "I love it!"

Brandon nodded. "I'm pretty good with naming stuff, and even *I* think that's pretty good."

Her Mom beamed. "Do you think? I just thought, you know, because we're kind of in this bay area and right on the water and...I don't know, it just fit."

Jade nodded. "It definitely fits."

There was a knock at the door and everyone looked at each other, slightly confused. Her mom stood up. "Who could that be, maybe one of Uncle Mike's friends who doesn't know he's gone?"

She went the front door and opened it; Jade could hear laughter and some chatter.

"Mom!" Jade called out. "Who is it?"

"Oh it's no one – I mean, not no one. No one that you know."

Jade and Brandon shot each other a look.

"Is it someone that we're *allowed* to know?" said Jade with a smile.

Her mom returned to the dining room followed by a large police officer. He had a mustache and a sort of frowny look on his face.

"Uh oh, your mom's new in town and she's already in trouble," said Brandon.

"Oh no, not at all," said the officer. "I was just stopping by to give your mom some information about her friend."

"What friend, Mom?" asked Jade.

"Ah, just someone I knew before you were born. Chief Hank, this is my middle daughter, Jade, and her husband, Brandon."

Chief Hank gave an awkward wave. "It's very nice to meet you both, I didn't mean to interrupt your dinner."

Jade shook her head. "There's not much to interrupt. We scarfed it down so quickly that it was more like sharks feeding than a dinner."

Everyone laughed.

Brandon reached towards the lasagna, "I'm not quite done yet," he said.

"Would you like to join us?" her mom asked.

Chief Hank shook his head. "No, I don't want to be a bother. I was just heading home and thought I would stop by."

"We don't bite," said Jade. "And we definitely can't eat all this lasagna on our own."

"No really, I've got to run."

Jade watched as her mom ran off to the kitchen and came back with a plastic container. "Well at least take some with you, and if it's not good, and you don't like it, you can just throw it away – I won't know the difference."

He laughed and accepted the container. "I'm sure it's delicious. Well, it was very nice meeting you all, I hope I'll be seeing more of you, and – have a nice evening!"

"You too," said Jade.

Brandon was already halfway through his second piece of lasagna and added a muffled goodbye. When her mom got back to the table, Jade asked her what friend she was talking about.

"Oh honey, it's someone that I knew years ago and I saw a picture of her here on the island and I thought that maybe the police would be able to look her up for me."

"Look her up? Is she a criminal?"

Her mom laughed. "No Jade, of course not. I promise that I'll tell you all about it if I ever get in contact with her family."

Jade cocked her head to the side. "Not in contact with *her*? Is she missing or something?"

"Oh, no, but – I'll just have to tell you the whole story later. Finish up your lasagna so I can give you a tour of the barn."

She cut herself a sliver of lasagna – she was stuffed, but she needed just one more taste.

"Okay!"

She decided to drop it for now, but there was definitely something weird about this friend. Or this Chief. Jade was determined to get it out of her mom sooner or later.

Chapter 4

After a quick tour of the barn and a short walk around the property, it was already time for Margie to drive Jade and Brandon back to the ferry terminal.

"That went so fast! Please come back soon. Or I can come to you! But I don't want to be a bother," she said as they drove to the east side of the island.

Jade laughed. "You could never be a bother, Mom. I think I'll come back next week. I can work from home a lot of the time, so maybe I can even stay with you once you get your internet up and running. I can work from the house and we can hang out."

"That would be great!" Margie found a spot to park and stopped the car. "Well, you two better get on the ferry so you don't get stuck on the island overnight."

Brandon laughed. "If I left the planning up to Jade, we would *definitely* get stuck here overnight."

Margie's jaw tensed. It was the only way she could keep herself from responding to Brandon's dig at Jade. No matter what Jade did (or didn't) do, Brandon could find some way to criticize her. It drove Margie insane, but her attempts to stop him in the past had failed. She learned that her only option was to keep quiet.

He unbuckled his seat belt. "Thanks again, I'm sure I'll be seeing you soon, too."

"Yes, anytime. Don't hesitate to pop over!"

Jade leaned over and gave her a kiss on the cheek before opening the car door. "Love you Mom! Have a good night!"

Margie sat in the car and watched as they made their way down the hill. She didn't want to leave until she saw them disappear safely onto the ferry. Even though her daughter was twenty-five years old, there were some habits that she just couldn't break.

Once she was satisfied that they made it on, Margie sat in the car and debated what to do next. It was a lovely night, and the idea of going back to her empty house seemed much too lonely. She decided that she would walk around Friday Harbor and take in the sights.

Margie got out of her car and strolled down the street. It was much livelier now than it was even a month before when she came to "buy" the property. As the weather warmed and summer vacations approached, more and more people would fill the island. It made her feel full of hope – not just for her future business, but for life in general.

Walking slowly, Margie enjoyed the music and laughter booming out from the restaurants along First Street. She stopped in front of a real estate agency window – they had printouts, with pictures, of local properties for sale. Margie could not believe the prices of some of these places. The houses were going for *millions* of dollars.

She got an uneasy feeling, wondering how much her brother's property was actually worth – she knew that he bought it many years ago, and it likely wasn't outrageously expensive at the time. But the truth was, it was a large piece of land with water access and beautiful views; he probably could have sold it for *at least* one million dollars, if not more.

Margie peered from picture to picture, hoping that she could find something that wasn't quite *that* expensive. No such luck. At least not for a property right on the water. It was obvious that her brother lost out on *a lot* of money by gifting her the barn and the house. He never much cared for money, and he never had a wife or family, so he was rather generous with them all. She decided that he probably felt sorry for her – something that she never intended.

After the divorce, the court determined that she was entitled to seven years of alimony. At the time, Margie felt strange taking the money from her newly ex-husband, but she had no other options. When they met in college, Margie was in school for engineering, but soon Jeff proposed to her and they were married. Margie became pregnant almost instantly and Jeff convinced her to put her schooling plans on hold so that he could focus on finishing his education and starting his business.

For the most part, it worked wonderfully. Jeff started an accounting business and was free to focus entirely on building it from the ground up. Margie was happy to raise the kids, take care of the home, and try to be Super Mom. It wasn't exactly what she planned for her life, but she loved being a mother. She loved being a wife. And she was darn good at it.

It was strange to her how cut and dried the divorce was – the judge simply took the number of years they were married, divided by three, and rounded down. Seven years of alimony for her to build a new life for herself.

Margie was forty-two years old at the time and she had no job history on her resume. She looked into going back to finish her credits for engineering, but it was unbelievably expensive. Tuition at the public university was more than $13,000 per year. She decided on going to community college to get a degree as a medical assistant.

That helped her become self-sufficient, sure, but by no means did it get her where she wanted to be. She thought she'd be able to save up enough to buy herself a small house, but the housing prices in Seattle had ballooned over the past twenty years.

It wasn't even that her kids were still in the area – once Connor went to college, she could have left and moved somewhere less expensive. But Seattle was home to all of them, and she wanted to keep it as home for them. At that she knew she failed.

Jeff ended up opening an accounting branch in New York City and he spent most of his time there. It wasn't his fault that they'd fallen out of love – he was quite civil about it all. He sat her down one day, took her by the hand, and told her that he would always love her but he couldn't be married to her anymore.

A breeze drifted through the streets and Margie felt a chill run down her spine. She should have brought a jacket, but she hadn't planned on being out this late. It was best to keep moving.

She took a left onto Spring Street; the road had a decent incline, which she hoped would get her heart rate up and get the blood flowing. She was moving a bit slowly to take in all the shops and restaurants along the street. There was a grocery store, a few storefronts for kayaking and whale watching tours, and a number of shops with knickknacks.

Margie loved knickknacks – she stared into the window of a store that was filled with San Juan Island dishtowels and aprons and other kitchen paraphernalia that she couldn't resist. She made a mental note to come back later this week when the stores were open.

After walking past the majority of the shops and stores, she came to a traffic circle. She wanted to keep going and see what else was nearby, but something caught her eye. On the edge of the traffic circle, there was a small parking lot and shopping plaza. On the sidewalk laid a pile of flowers and what looked like a poster. Margie carefully made her way there to see what this was about. When she got close, her heart sunk.

In memory of Kelly Allen, beloved wife, mother, sister and daughter.

The same picture that was in the newspaper stared back at her now, Kelly's laughing face and big brown eyes. Margie took a step back. It was still shocking to see Kelly's face. She had only seen her once before, twenty-three years ago...and she looked very different then.

The night they met was a Sunday, and a dark and stormy one at that. Margie had just had Connor, and that night was another struggle to chase the two older children around the house and into bed. Jeff was away on business, as he often was back in those days, trying to get things off the ground.

Margie had finally gotten the kids to bed and hadn't heard any little feet creeping downstairs for almost an hour when there was a knock at the door. She ran to answer it as quickly as she could; she didn't need this person waking the kids and forcing her to start the bedtime ordeal all over again.

When she opened the door, she saw a small, frightened looking young woman, her dark hair soaking wet. Margie was struck by the wild look in her eyes.

"Yes? Can I help you?"

The woman stared back at her but didn't say a word.

Margie leaned closer. "Are you okay?"

"Is this...Jeff Clifton's house?"

"Yes, I'm Margie Clifton. Have we met before?"

The woman shook her head. "No, we haven't. Actually – this is a mistake. I have to go."

Margie watched as the girl turned and swiftly walked down the sidewalk.

She ran after her. "Young lady! You can't go out in this storm. Please come inside, I can help you call a cab or something."

The girl stopped and turned around. She looked tortured.

"Please. I insist."

The girl finally agreed to come inside. Her clothes were completely drenched. When she was in the light, Margie thought that she looked like a high school student.

"Hang on a second, I'll grab you some dry clothes and make some tea. Then we can get you back home, okay?"

The girl nodded. Margie went upstairs and heard Connor crying. Of course – it was time for him to get a bottle. She gathered some dry clothes and picked Connor up from his bassinet. When she got back to the front door, the girl was nowhere to be seen. Margie wondered if, in her sleep deprived state, she'd imagined her. But she quickly found her, sitting at the kitchen counter, staring off into space.

"Here – you can change into these. There's a bathroom right over there."

The girl accepted the clothes without a word and went to the bathroom. Margie prepared a bottle for Connor and was already feeding him by the time she returned.

"You can set your wet things there – I can even throw them in the dryer once I finish feeding Connor if you'd like."

The girl shook her head and stared at Connor with wide eyes. "No, that's okay."

"Are you – do you go to the school nearby? Fairview High?"

"No. I'm a freshman. At Portland State."

"Oh, okay. I had some friends go there. You're far from home."

The girl nodded and stood up as though she were going to leave. "Listen – thank you for everything, but I have to go."

"If you're in some sort of trouble, I can help you."

She stood for a moment, biting her lip. "I'm pregnant. And – I'd like you to take the baby."

Margie's jaw dropped. That certainly wasn't what she expected. "Well – I mean, I just had a baby of my own. And I have two others. This is quite touching, but I'm sure that you can find..."

"Jeff is the father. Jeff is the father of my baby. I haven't told anyone."

If Margie wasn't already sitting down, she would've fallen over. "Excuse me? What did you say?"

"I didn't know that he...was married. I just found out, and..."

"You must have him confused with another Jeff," said Margie, her voice rising. Jeff always told her that as his business became more successful, they would need to be careful of people trying to scam them. His voice flashed in her mind. *"We can't let people think that we're suckers, right?"*

"I'm not confused," the girl said softly. "He's lying to you. You should leave him, you shouldn't let him –"

"My husband is not lying to me. We have been happily married for five years."

Connor started to cry. Margie popped him on her shoulder, trying for a burp.

"I'm sorry," the girl said before grabbing her wet clothes and running out the front door.

The next morning, Margie wondered if she dreamt it all. She ran through the conversation in her head again and again. Was it possible that it was all in her head?

But in the bathroom, she found a keychain. It was just a name – Kelly, on a miniature license plate, probably picked up on a road trip somewhere. It didn't make any sense. Jeff was a good man – a great man. He was a wonderful father. Why would he do something as irresponsible as having an affair with an eighteen-year-old girl? It made no sense.

Margie was afraid to even bring it up at risk of insulting him. The most she dared to do was tell him that a young woman named Kelly dropped by looking for him.

"I don't think I know a Kelly," he said evenly. "Did she say what she wanted?"

"No," replied Margie. "Just stopped by to say hello."

She watched him carefully, and he didn't react in the slightest. It was as though she'd told him that the mailman stopped by. She tucked the keychain away in her jewelry box, deciding that she'd think it over again later once she wasn't as exhausted with taking care of the baby.

Yet later never came. The kids were young and needy; Margie honestly forgot about the whole ordeal. Until recently.

Margie reached into her pocket and pulled out the keychain, running her fingers over the letters. Was it some coincidence that fate brought her back to this island and reconnected her with this woman?

A single drop of water hit Margie on the nose. She looked up, just as a bolt of lightning flashed across the sky.

Chapter 5

The sun was still rising as Morgan made her way to the bike rental place. All she had with her was a backpack – she wanted to travel light. She climbed the steps to the storefront and peered into the windows. It was dark and no one was inside.

What in the world? What kind of business isn't open early in the morning?

Leaning back, she looked at the store hours in the window. "They don't open until *nine*!"

She groaned. Maybe this was that island time thing people always laughed about. It wasn't funny to her, though. She pulled out her phone and searched for a taxi company. There didn't seem to be anything on San Juan Island – no taxi, no Uber, no nothing. How odd – it was like she'd gone back in time.

It was more than nine miles to get to where she was going, and so far, nothing was going to plan. She missed the first ferry into Friday Harbor and had to wait an hour for the next one. Now her admittedly weak plan for transportation was sabotaged.

It didn't matter. Nothing would stop her. She put the address into her phone and started walking.

The route wasn't too bad at first, but the road quickly ran out of sidewalk. She found herself squeezing onto the shoulder of a two lane road where drivers went way too fast for her comfort. Maybe there was a bus? She stopped and checked her phone – nothing. At least nothing that Google could find for her.

With a sigh, she tucked her phone into her back pocket and decided to retie her shoe before she kept going. From behind, she heard a car slowing down. The muscles in her legs and back tensed.

"Do you need a ride?" called out a voice.

Morgan turned around to see a small SUV with mountain bikes on top and four passengers stuffed inside. A ride would solve about *half* of her problems at the moment. But at the same time, she'd never hitchhiked before, and it didn't seem like a *great* idea. On the other hand, these people looked young and nice – not at all like they'd kill a hitchhiker.

"Where are you headed?" she asked.

"We were going to check out Mount Finlayson. It's just up the road."

"I'm headed to Cattle Point."

"Well that's not far from where we're going," said the woman in the passenger seat. "Are you going for a hike? Would you like a ride there?"

A hike. Ha. Morgan bit her lip. It would save her a lot of time and these people seemed normal. How different was it from Uber? Except that it was free.

"I'd really appreciate it, if you don't mind," she finally said.

"Hop on in!"

Morgan climbed into the back seat, squishing the two passengers who were already there. She introduced herself, and they told her that they were in for the holiday weekend – camping by Lime Kiln on the other side of the island.

"That sounds really nice," said Morgan.

The woman up front turned around to join the conversation. "It's been awesome so far. If you're staying out that way, feel free to stop by our campsite. Usually by dark, we're all exhausted just hanging out, listening to the sounds of the water."

Morgan smiled. That sounded peaceful. But she didn't feel peaceful – not that they needed to know that. "Yeah thanks, I'll keep that in mind."

It only took them about seven minutes to get her to the Cattle Point Trail. It was a much nicer option than the three hour walk that she'd committed herself to. She got out of the car and thanked them for the ride; they reversed and drove away, waving.

First hitchhiking experience – five stars.

What was most surprising to her was that she was the only one on this hiking trail. She stood and stared at the lighthouse on the tip of Cattle Point. Tall grasses swayed with an immaculate view of the water and other islands in the distance. She stood as the wind blew in her ears, soaking in the stark difference of the warm car, filled with people and smiles, and her standing here at what felt like the edge of the world.

Had her mom ever hiked this trail? Did she like the view? Morgan would never get the chance to ask her...

That was enough. She had places to be and people to harass.

Taking a peek at her phone, she found the road that she needed to follow and started walking. It was surprisingly easy to find it online – there really was no privacy with the internet. It only took about ten minutes to get to the house, and then she was faced with a long, private driveway.

She decided that she should try to be as inconspicuous as possible, especially since it was now light out. Instead of walking on the actual driveway, she walked about ten feet to the side through some trees and brush. It wasn't too bad and she felt like she was pretty well hidden. She spotted a large garage at the back of the property. Before she went to check it out, she waited for about five minutes to make sure that there was no movement within the house.

When she was satisfied that she was alone, she crept to the side of the garage to investigate the door there. She tried the handle – no luck. It was locked. She leaned up against the nearest window and peered inside. The garage was enormous. There were eight cars, some of them lifted above the others.

"Rich people," she muttered. She'd never seen anything like it in her life. There was one car covered up by some sort of a tarp. That could be the one she needed.

She spent the next fifteen minutes trying to pick the lock like she'd read about online. Once that failed, she tried to find some other way to sneak into this garage. It was surprisingly locked down.

She was about to leave and come back later that night with a better lock picking strategy when she heard the whoop of a police siren.

Oh boy.

"Morning," called out the officer.

Morgan stood frozen in her tracks. Some panicked thoughts raced through her mind – should she run? How far would she get? How cold was the water in the ocean? Probably pretty cold, but...

He walked up to her. "Mind telling me what you're doing here?"

"I was – on a hike. And I got lost."

The officer frowned. "Do you always go hiking in white sneakers?"

Morgan looked down at her feet, then back up to him. He was a big guy – not fat, but not skinny. He was just a *big* dude. She wondered if he was a fast runner. She certainly wasn't...

"Yeah, these are old," she finally said.

"Is there a reason that you were playing with the handle on his door here?"

"What, this? Oh," she laughed nervously. "I just wanted to see the cars inside. They look really nice."

They looked really nice! What!

He nodded, looking around. "Well, the owner of those nice cars doesn't want you poking around here. So I'm going to have to remove you for trespassing. Do you have some identification?"

She groaned. "Yes sir. It's in my backpack. Is it okay if I grab it?"

"Oh sure, but do it slowly."

She nodded and removed the bag from her back at almost a sloth like pace.

"Not so fast!" he yelled.

She threw her hands up. "Sorry!"

He laughed. "Just kidding, that was fine. Go ahead."

Morgan's heart pounded in her chest. Did he really just make a joke? She was too stunned to absorb it. She carefully unzipped the top pocket of the bag and pulled out her driver's license.

He accepted it, squinted at it, then held it out further from his face.

"You've got to be kidding me," he said under his breath.

"I'm not kidding sir." Morgan had her hands up again.

"No – put your hands down." He rubbed his face with his hand. "You're Morgan Allen?"

"Yes sir."

The front door of the house opened and a man popped his head out. "That's the one! Arrest her!"

"Crabs on a cracker," muttered the officer. "Go back in your home, *now*."

"I don't want her –"

"Now!" He yelled.

Morgan realized for the first time how cold her hands were. She stared at the man in the doorway, her mouth hanging open.

He stared back at them for a moment before slamming the door.

The officer turned back to her. "Okay kid, we'll talk more in the car. Let's go. Do you have a bike or something?"

She shook her head.

"How'd you get here?"

She wrinkled her nose – she knew that she shouldn't lie to an officer, but she really didn't want to tell the truth. "I – caught a ride with some people."

"Oh. Okay. Take a seat in the back."

Heart thundering away, Morgan sat in the back of the police car. She'd never been in a police car before. Trespassing wasn't that bad, was it? Was she going to go to jail or something?

"I'm Hank, the Chief Deputy Sheriff."

Morgan felt a fingernail digging into her palm from her tightly clasped hands. She made herself loosen her grip. "So you're the top guy?"

He shook his head. "No. You're thinking of the sheriff."

"Oh, okay."

"But I'd still like you to tell me what you are actually doing out here. And don't tell me that you were hiking."

Morgan felt dizzy. She never thought her plan was the smartest, and now she was afraid to even say it out loud. "It's – well I wasn't really thinking."

"I can see that."

She continued. "I was looking for a car – one car in particular."

Hank crossed his arms. "Was it a 1963 Corvette Sting Ray?"

Oh shoot. He knew *exactly* who she was and *exactly* what she was doing. She closed her eyes. "Yes."

"You're looking for the car that hit your mom and left its bumper behind?"

She kept her eyes closed – she could feel the tears coming. "Yes."

Hank let out a sigh. "I know that this may not sound like much, but we've looked everywhere for that car."

"I just thought that there might be a clue or something..."

He was silent.

She opened her eyes and leaned forward to see what he was doing. He was just sitting there with one hand on the steering wheel, staring forward.

"Listen kid. I know that this feels like the right thing to do, but it's not the right thing to do. Brock Hunter is a dangerous man, and for more than just his drunk driving record. I don't want you going on his property again, or I will really have to arrest you. It's for your own good."

Morgan took a deep breath and looked out the window. She tried to steady her voice before answering. "Okay."

"I'm serious. Tell me that you won't go back there."

"I won't go back."

"Okay, good." He started the car. "We have an understanding. Now where are you staying?"

He was changing the subject. Good. "I haven't figured that out yet. I was hoping I could find some place to camp, or maybe a hotel room to rent."

He turned around. "Are you kidding me?"

She shook her head. "I haven't kidded you this entire time!"

He rubbed his forehead. "Well, I can confidently say that there is probably not a single place left on the island that isn't booked this weekend."

"Oh."

Planning was never really her forte.

"Do you want me to drive you back to the ferry?"

"Well, I was hoping to stay for a bit. I want to visit the place where my mom..." Her voice started to crack. "Well, and just some other stuff."

"Ah. I see."

He sat for a moment before continuing. "Well, if you've got an open mind, I think I know a lady who's got a place for you to stay."

She sat up straight. "Really?"

"You bet," he said as he reversed out of the driveway.

Chapter 6

Maybe he should call first? No – even if he wanted to, he didn't have Margie's number.

Yet.

He glanced in the rear view mirror. Morgan sat still, clutching her backpack to her chest and looking out the window. She reminded him of his own daughter – except his daughter was a more skilled liar. It served her well in her marketing career now, but it drove him crazy when she was a teenager.

Hank didn't have a backup plan if Margie wasn't home, or if she wouldn't let this girl, who was essentially a stranger, into her home. He could offer her a place to sleep in the county jail, but that seemed horrible. What was she thinking, coming out here and trying to break into Brock Hunter's garage? Did she really think that the police had been so negligent that they hadn't thought to look there?

Of course they'd looked. They looked everywhere. When Morgan's mother was found, badly injured, and taken to the hospital, all that was left at the crash site was a back bumper. The driver of the car presumably hit Kelly Allen, then reversed into a pole, and drove off without their bumper. Unfortunately, there was no license plate.

Brock was one of the richest men on the island, and he definitely believed that he was above the law. He was the only one on San Juan who had a car that matched that bumper, but that wasn't enough proof. Hank suspected that he must have worked extremely quickly to get the damaged car smuggled off of the island. It was probably destroyed within twelve hours of the accident.

Brock was arrested that evening for a DUI. Oddly, he was driving a 2001 Toyota Camry – a vehicle that was far beneath his wealth and pride. One of their best deputies questioned the owner of that vehicle – a mechanic who lived on the mainland. But he offered no explanation for his car mysteriously appearing on San Juan Island in the control of Brock Hunter.

While it seemed obvious that Brock was the culprit, they had no hard evidence. Morgan was right to be suspicious of Brock, but she was too young to understand how easily a rich man could slip from the fingers of justice.

Yes, in an ideal world the love of a young woman for her mother would be enough to solve the case. But Hank knew all too well the special level of justice that the very rich experienced – and Brock was no exception. He wasn't even convicted of the DUI from that night – his lawyer was able to get him out of it, despite a blood test showing that he was at two and a half times the legal limit.

The entire sheriff's department was still looking for evidence – still going after leads. But Hank didn't want to get the poor girl's hopes up. It didn't look good.

He cleared his throat. "Have you ever been to San Juan before?"

"No. This is my first visit."

"Oh." Not the best first visit, but okay.

"My parents were here for a, uh, anniversary trip. My mom kept sending me pictures and telling me how beautiful it was..."

"I'm very sorry about your mom. The entire community has been mourning and we still are working on the case."

"Thank you."

He looked in the rear view mirror again to see that she was back to looking out the window. He decided not to say anything else. He knew firsthand that the things people said to someone grieving were often less helpful than intended.

They drove the rest of the way in silence, with Hank growing increasingly more nervous about this scheme that occurred to him. Maybe this really *wasn't* a good idea. Was he just trying to find an excuse to stop by and see Margie again? Margie was so unbelievably hospitable when he stopped by to give her Morgan's name – surely she would be even more excited to see the girl herself!

No. This was a bad idea.

But it was too late.

With any luck, she wouldn't be home. Hank slowly ascended the driveway and it occurred to him that he needed to bring back Margie's plastic container. The lasagna she gave him the other night was heavenly – absolutely heavenly. He decided that it was better he didn't have the container now, because it gave him another excuse to stop by.

He pulled up in front of the house and parked the car. Before he could tell Morgan to stay in the car, she already opened the door and hopped out.

Should've locked the doors. Well, it seemed that this was happening.

He walked up to the front door and rang the doorbell; Morgan stood a few feet behind him. Hank looked back at her and smiled. Could she tell that he was being a bit insane?

The front door opened and there stood Margie, with bits of paint splattered and speckled onto her face and shirt. "Oh! Chief Hank! Hi!"

"Hey Margie, sorry to interrupt your –"

She laughed. "It's no trouble at all. What's going on?"

"Well, I got a call about a trespasser this morning and you'll never guess who it was." He stepped to the side and watched Margie's face carefully.

It looked like a little gust of wind hit her. Her eyebrows went up and her entire body appeared to sway slightly backwards, but the smile remained frozen on her face.

Morgan stepped forward, hand outstretched. "It's very nice to meet you, my name is Morgan Allen."

"It's very nice to meet you too, I'm Margie Clifton."

Hank's eyes darted between them both. "Uh, Margie used to know your mom. Back in the day."

"Oh really?" said Morgan, her eyes brightening.

Margie nodded rapidly. "Yes, very briefly, more than twenty years ago. I saw her picture and...well, I'm just so very sorry for your loss sweetheart."

Morgan offered a pained smile.

"Well," Hank said, putting his hands on his hips. "The reason that I brought her here – well, she can tell you more about that. But I had the choice of arresting her or helping her find a place to stay on the island. Everything right now is booked, and I thought – and I'm realizing now how silly this sounds – that maybe if you had –"

Margie threw her hands up. "Of course! Yes, I have plenty of room! I would be happy to host you."

"I really don't want to impose," said Morgan. "Once a place opens up on the island, I'll book it right away. I might just find a campsite or something."

"It's no problem at all. As long as you don't mind me painting and trying to spruce some things up."

"I'd be happy to help actually," said Morgan.

"Would you look at that," said Hank. "You just doubled your workforce."

Margie let out a small laugh and Hank cringed – he really put her in a tough position. Why hadn't he turned the car around when he had the chance? It seemed like he was taking advantage of her kindness, but it wasn't his intention at all. He had this strange urge to see her again, and he knew that she wanted to meet this girl and...well, it lead him to this misguided situation.

"If you don't have the room, I'm sure I can find somewhere for her," said Hank. That wasn't true of course, but he needed to at least offer it.

"No no, please don't. It'd be nice to have someone else around here."

Before he could stop himself, Hank said, "Oh, is your husband not staying with you?"

Margie scrunched her shoulders up and down a quick motion. "Nope! My ex-husband lives in New York City."

Hank's stomach did a little twirl. Ex-husband!

"That's so cool," said Morgan. "I always wanted to visit New York City. Have you been there?"

Margie nodded. "Yes, we went there several times when we were married – he was setting up a new branch of his business there. It's certainly a charming city, though I've never been much of a city girl."

"Me neither," said Morgan.

"That makes three of us!" said Hank. "I'm just like you country girls."

Now they both laughed – actually laughed. He decided to leave before any other bizarre things escaped from his mouth.

"Well, I'd better be getting back to work now. Morgan – remember what I told you. And Margie – it was a pleasure, as always."

Morgan nodded, lips pursed tightly together.

"Of course!" said Margie with a smile. "Thanks again Chief Hank. See you later."

"I hope so," he said.

Hank promptly turned around and walked towards his car, his eyes tightly shut. What had gotten into him? He was acting like a giddy schoolgirl. He hadn't felt this way in...well, who knows how long. Yet every time that he saw her, he liked her more and more. She had a wonderful energy – she sucked him in. It was more than just the cooking. It was more than her being cute. She reminded him of the sun somehow and she made him feel...hopeful?

What was that? He got into his car and shook his head. Hopeful. That was something he hadn't felt in years.

But just because Margie was like a human ray of sunshine, it didn't mean that she deserved to have his grumpiness following her around the island. The poor woman had only been in town for a few days and she already had to see his face four times.

Hank started the car. It was best to leave her alone. He needed to get back to his regular life. Work. Dinners at the pizza shop. Quiet nights at the house.

And while it wasn't the kind of life that his wife told him she wanted him to have before she passed away, it was the only life that felt right to him. How could he be happy again after she was gone? It seemed wrong. It hadn't even crossed his mind until recently.

That was it. He needed to get back to normal. He reversed down the driveway and set his mind to focusing on work. Maybe he could actually get Morgan the justice she deserved.

Chapter 7

Margie could hear Hank's car rolling down the driveway as she closed the front door. She turned around and faced the girl.

"Well! I'm finishing up painting one of the bedrooms, and I just need to run to the restroom first, so I'll be right back."

"Okay," replied Morgan.

Margie smiled and then quickly made her way to the bathroom. It wasn't entirely true, of course, that she needed to rush off right then. Somehow she managed to keep up a coherent conversation until now, but she didn't think it could last. She was still in shock – she couldn't remember *what* she'd been saying! Maybe she *wasn't* making sense!

She got to the bathroom and closed the door. What on earth had she gotten herself into? Yes, she wanted to know more about Kelly Allen. And yes, she thought that someday, she might reach out to Kelly's kid and...what? Ask her if she ever wondered who her father was?

Margie sat down on the toilet. Her mouth was dry and her hands were sweaty. The last time that Hank stopped by, she'd only gotten Morgan's name. She didn't get a picture of the girl, and certainly not the girl herself.

She looked so...well, she looked shockingly like Jade. That was the most jarring – it struck her all at once. She had Jade's eyes. She also had the same long dark hair as Jade, but they were close in age and Margie reasoned that it was just how girls in their twenties wore their hair.

It didn't mean that they were related. It was entirely possible that Kelly was confused all those years ago – or perhaps that she was lying. There were a hundred possibilities that explained it all without completely turning her life upside down.

Margie flushed the toilet – for appearance's sake – and took a look at herself in the mirror. Her skin was a bit pale, but she doubted that anyone would notice that. She washed her hands and dabbed her face with a towel.

This was not how she expected her day to go, but she couldn't just turn this poor girl away. Though...did Hank say something about trespassing? Or did she imagine that?

It didn't matter. What mattered was that this young woman recently lost her mother – a woman who Margie met over twenty years ago, and they didn't leave on the best terms. Maybe the poor woman really did just need some help that night. And whatever the truth was, whatever Kelly's reasons were for showing up, Margie regretted how their conversation went. That night haunted her.

And though it felt like all of this was happening quite suddenly, with Morgan literally showing up on her doorstep, for Margie it was over twenty years of wondering. It was time for her to figure it out.

Margie left the bathroom and found Morgan just where she left her. The poor girl must be frightened, she decided – going from the back of a police car to a stranger's home.

"Well! I must say it's very exciting for me to have a guest. I only just moved in here a few days ago."

"You have a beautiful home," said Morgan, her hands clasped tightly in front of her. "I'd be happy to help with any painting or projects that you're working on."

"That's very nice of you, but you certainly don't have to –"

"Or of course I could pay rent. Or – like a hotel room fee?"

Margie laughed. "Please don't worry yourself with that. Would you like something to drink? Or eat? I do have some leftovers in the fridge."

"I would love some water," said Morgan.

"I'll grab you a glass, and then how about I give you the tour?"

"That would be great!"

Margie filled a glass with water and handed it to Morgan before leading her around the house – showing her where everything was in the kitchen, how to work the television in the living room, and each of the four bedrooms.

"Right now only my bedroom and one of the spare bedrooms actually has a bed in it. I'm running pretty low on furniture around here. And I also wanted to buy a bunch of chairs for the barn. Oh! Let me show you the barn next."

Margie led her outside and told her about the rest of the property, explaining how her brother sold it to her and her plans for the barn.

"I went to the website for permits the other day, and I couldn't make heads or tails of it. I need to find out if there is an office in town that could help me."

"I can help with that!" Morgan said, uncrossing her arms. "Please let me help, I would feel really bad staying here without doing something in return."

Margie smiled. She did seem like a very sweet girl. Kelly raised her well. Margie felt a small tug of guilt, which she tried to ignore. "You know, that would actually be a huge help. I much prefer painting furniture to filling out forms online."

"Then I'm your girl!"

They went back inside and as Margie finished painting, Morgan got on the computer for two hours, printing out forms and instructions.

Over the next few days, her anxiety surrounding Morgan melted. Margie decided it was best not to pry or ask anything about Morgan's personal life – if Morgan wanted to share, she would. Instead, she focused on utilizing her help in getting the house and barn up to speed. Morgan proved to be quite the little helper and cheerful companion.

Morgan spent an entire day helping Margie clean up a few messes left behind in the barn by some of the workers that Mike hired. She took the time to read and understand all of the permit forms that they needed – she even went into town to make sure she had it all right. They filled them out together, and Margie felt confident that they were on the right track.

Mid week, Margie caught wind of a liquidation sale at a wedding venue on the mainland.

"Look at all of these nice things that they're getting rid of," she said to Morgan, showing her the pictures online. "I could really use a lot of this. The tables, all of these nice gold painted chairs."

Morgan was immediately interested. "We could rent a U-Haul truck and buy everything that we can fit in there."

Margie frowned. "But we have to rent that on the mainland, and how would we get to the U-Haul station? Would we leave the car there? Can we do that? And then ferry back to get it..."

"No problem! We park here, in Friday Harbor. We take the ferry over and I'll order an Uber. It will actually work once we get back off of the island."

"Isn't that...dangerous?" asked Margie.

Morgan shrugged. "Not really. Isn't everything dangerous if you think too much about it?"

"I guess," Margie said with a laugh.

The next day, they walked onto the ferry, made the ride to Anacortes, and Morgan ordered an Uber to pick them up from the ferry terminal. Margie felt a bit nervous as they waited, but after a few minutes, a nice lady about her age pulled up to get them.

"Morgan?" she asked.

Morgan nodded. "Carol?"

"Oh this is much better than I expected!" whispered Margie. Morgan smiled.

It was just over a ten minute drive to pick up the truck; Margie was anxious to start the two hour trip.

"Are you sure that you don't want me to drive?" asked Morgan.

"Oh I'm sure. Every time we moved, I was always the driver. Plus it's just a little bit bigger than the minivan that we used to have." Margie laughed, remembering that she often felt like a bus driver throughout the years.

"It's probably for the better. My dad says that I'm a bad driver."

"Oh?" Margie couldn't stop herself from asking a few questions now. "Where is your dad?"

"Oh, he's back in Portland."

"Does he know that you're staying on the island?"

Morgan bit her lip. "Not exactly. He knows that I took a break from school. And he knows that I was staying with some friends in Seattle..."

"I see."

"I mean, he wouldn't be upset or anything. Well, he would be, but not because he doesn't want me to be here. He'd just worry."

"Well that *is* a parent's main job." Margie suppressed a smile.

Morgan sighed. "I know. I'm just trying not to worry him."

"Well, I still think that you should be honest with him."

"I know," Morgan said with a nod. "I will be."

It felt like a weight came off of Margie's chest. Morgan had a dad! And the poor man was worried about her and waiting for her to go back to school, but he existed, and it wasn't Jeff!

Margie's spirits were high for the rest of the trip. Traffic and rain didn't bother her one bit. They got to the liquidation place and bought a bunch of tables, chairs, table cloths and centerpieces. The prices were unreal – when she'd looked at buying some of these things new, the cost was five times as much! And everything was in great condition.

It didn't escape Margie that this place must have failed in a spectacular way to have to sell off all of this new and nice stuff, but she tried not to let it worry her. Even if her business failed, maybe she could get a job as a medical assistant at a doctor's office on the island.

They packed the truck almost entirely full and made their way back to the ferry. It was an all day endeavor, and by the time they got the truck back to Saltwater Cove, they were exhausted. They managed to unload everything but left the task of returning the truck for the next day.

"I need to make us some dinner!" Margie announced once they were finally back in the house.

"No please, let me. I bought the ingredients at the grocery store yesterday and I was hoping to make dinner for you for once."

"Well isn't that nice."

Margie settled onto a stool at the kitchen bar, sipping on a cup of tea. This day couldn't have gone any better. Everything she'd gotten for the barn was a steal, she found out that Morgan had a father, and it seemed like she and Morgan found one another at just the right time.

It still felt like fate brought them together for a reason – perhaps more than just buying furniture and painting rooms. And Margie was determined for her relationship with Morgan to go better than her relationship with Kelly.

Chapter 8

On Friday, Jade was able to get all of her work done before noon. To her surprise, when she sent her most recent project off to her boss, she got an email back saying that she should take the rest of the day off and get an early start on her weekend. This was sent in an email, though, so Jade felt like she should double check with her in person.

She knocked softly on her boss's open door. "Hey, do you have a second?"

Madeleine waved her in. "Of course! Come on in. I was just looking over your email."

"Does everything look okay?"

"Yes, as always. It looks great."

"Oh, okay good."

"I thought that you'd be out the door already," said Madeleine, leaning back in her chair.

"I just wanted to make sure that you didn't need anything else, and I really appreciate –"

"No, no. I'm all set. You did a great job on this, and I have plenty of time to review it before we have to present it on Wednesday. Seriously, go! I'm sure you're dying to get out to the island to see your mom."

"Okay! Thank you so much! If you need anything else please let me know."

"Have a good weekend."

Jade felt much better leaving now. She'd never gotten into trouble in the two years she'd been with the bank, but she always worried that just around the corner there would be a project that she couldn't do or data that she didn't understand.

Jade went to school to be a statistician and ended up learning a lot of different computer programming languages along the way. It was never her intent, but the programs were extremely useful to crunch large sets of data. She loved numbers and she loved solving problems, but since much of her programming knowledge was self-taught, she was always worried that soon the demands of her job would outstrip her skills and she would be seen as the fraud that she was.

She got back to the apartment and quickly packed a bag. Brandon wasn't home – he was working a shift at the grocery store where he was a part-time manager. They'd agreed that Brandon would just do some part-time hours so that he could put more time and effort into his DJ'ing business.

Jade didn't mind being the primary breadwinner – she wanted to support Brandon's dreams. Plus, she really loved her job, even though she always felt like she was a bit under qualified, especially for the large salary they paid her.

Brandon said that she should have negotiated an even higher salary when she started, but she thought it was already too much to begin with. Her boss also gave her two raises since she started – neither of which Jade asked for. Though she was grateful, and she knew that it was supposed to mean that she was doing a good job, it also worried her that she may not meet their expectations. She used that fear to fuel continued study in her free time.

After getting to the ferry terminal early, Jade got onto the ship with plenty of time and started to feel herself relax. It was a cloudy day, and she spent the entire trip on the outside deck. She had a cup of coffee to keep her warm, plus she was excited to meet her mom's newest tenant.

Jade got a somewhat scattered and brief overview of who this person was – it sounded like Chief Hank brought her by when she had nowhere to stay. It was so like her mom to take someone in like that. Growing up, all of Jade's friends used to love coming over because her mom showered them with attention, love, and of course lots of freshly baked cookies. Her best friend Katie started calling her "second Mom."

Her mom was waiting to pick her up from the ferry terminal, and Jade was a bit disappointed that the girl wasn't there too.

"Where's Melinda?"

Her mom laughed. "Her name is Morgan."

"Oh, right."

"And she's back at the barn. I've been waiting all day for the plumber to show up to finish hooking up the bathrooms, so she volunteered to stay behind and wait for him."

"Bathrooms? That's pretty cool."

"We *have* to have bathrooms! The barn can comfortably seat 220 people – and your uncle Mike started the process of adding bathrooms, but we had to finish a few details. Like the actual plumbing."

"Minor plumbing details. This is turning into quite an operation."

"I know," her mom said with a sigh. "To be honest, I'm not even really sure that this is going to work out."

"Why not? Are you running out of funding? I'd be happy to invest in this business," Jade said with a smile.

"Oh you stop it," her mom replied. "No, I was able to get a small business loan to get things up and running. But things do need to get off the ground in the next few months, so I can start paying the loan back."

"I'm sure that it'll all be fine. Now tell me about this girl who's living with you. Is she some sort of con artist?"

Her mom gave her a stern look. "Why would you say something like that! She's a very nice young woman. She's just a little...lost right now, I think."

"It's a very con artist thing to have a sob story," Jade said with a smile. She was kidding...mostly. But she didn't want her mom to be taken advantage of – a chronic problem for overly nice people.

"It's not a sob story. Her mom was that lady that I knew, very briefly, years ago. The lady who was killed by the hit and run driver."

"Oh! Well now I feel bad. I just wanted to make sure that, you know, it wasn't anything weird."

"I know honey. But don't worry about me. We've actually been having a great week. Did you get those pictures that I sent of all the nice chairs that we got for the barn?"

"I did! And I'm excited to see them in person."

When they pulled up to the house, they found the plumber's truck parked out front and headed straight to the barn. He was already hard at work, but Morgan was nowhere to be found.

Jade didn't get a chance to meet her until they went into the house; she was hauling a large laundry basket filled with linens.

"Morgan, this is my daughter Jade. Jade, this is Morgan."

"Nice to meet you." Morgan set down the laundry basket and offered a handshake.

"Nice to meet you, too. My mom is really putting you to work, isn't she?"

Morgan laughed. "Not really. I had to sneak this in while she was away."

"Are these some of the tablecloths that you got from that place?" asked Jade.

Morgan nodded. "I think they washed pretty nicely, so that's a good sign."

Her mom leaned over and inspected the basket. "Yeah, they do wash pretty well. But I will definitely need to iron them before we fold them. They're already getting wrinkly."

"I can iron them!" said Morgan. "I was thinking I could spread some towels on the kitchen table and iron them here – they're just too big to do anywhere else."

"Can't you guys get some kind of laundry service for these?" asked Jade. "You'll spend half of your time washing tablecloths and ironing them."

Her mom shrugged. "Maybe down the line. But for now, I'm trying to see how much I can do myself."

"Okay, that makes sense. I mean, I don't even iron any of my clothes at home, so I couldn't imagine ironing this. But whatever floats your boat." Jade crossed her arms. "So Morgan, is this your first time in the San Juans?"

"Uh, yes, it is."

"How do you like it so far?"

"I love it. It's gorgeous. I actually came here because of my mom." She cleared her throat. "She loved it here. She passed away a few months ago. On the island, actually. And it's been really nice to have something to keep myself busy."

Shoot – Jade hadn't meant to bring that up. Not at all. "My mom told me, and I'm so sorry to hear about that."

"It's okay. Actually, when I came here – well, when I first came to the island – it was because they still don't know who it was that hit her. With the car. The driver left behind a bumper, and there's only one person who has a car on the island that matches that bumper. The police made the mistake of telling my dad that so...I sort of tried to break into his garage to look for the car."

"Oh my goodness!"

Jade suppressed a smile. Her mom's mouth popped open almost instantly. "Calm down Mom. I would do the same thing if it was you."

Morgan continued. "I know it sounds stupid...and that's because it was. But they have the bumper from him and I don't know why they need any more evidence. Well, I guess I *do* know, I just wish that they could arrest him."

Jade frowned. "That's really tough. I'm so sorry."

"He was caught drunk driving later that night – in a different car. It's all very suspicious. But they stopped giving us updates months ago, and it felt like the case went cold. I just couldn't stand that."

Jade didn't want to make the poor girl talk about anything that she didn't want to talk about, but she was being very open about all of this.

"Do you have any siblings? Are they...involved too?"

Morgan shook her head. "No, it's just me and my dad. Well, he's my stepdad, technically, but he raised me since I was two years old."

"Oh – are your parents divorced?" asked Jade.

"No, my biological dad died before I was born. So I guess technically I'm an orphan," Morgan said with a weak laugh.

"You are *not* an orphan!" Jade's mom jumped in. "Your dad loves you *very* much and he's *very* worried about you. And you should *really* tell him where you've been."

Morgan nodded. "Yeah, I know. He'll just worry. And I kind of ended up here on a whim. It's – uh – kind of my thing."

Despite her mom's stern tone, it did seem to cheer Morgan up a bit. Poor girl – Jade now felt guilty that she ever even joked about her being a con artist.

Jade heard her phone ringing in her purse. She reached in to grab it.

"Speaking of dads, mine is calling right now." Jade stepped into one of the bedrooms and closed the door. "Hello?"

"Happy birthday sweetie!"

She frowned. "Dad, this is Jade."

There was silence for a moment. "Oh! I meant to call…"

"Tiffany, your *other* daughter!" Jade started laughing. "And her birthday is tomorrow."

"Of course, I knew that."

Jade shook her head. Her dad was never great on details, but it was really unfair. Her mom had always taken care of all that stuff for him. It really couldn't be helped at this point.

Jade was glad that he called, actually, because they didn't get a chance to talk often. Her dad didn't really like talking on the phone, but since she had him now, she excitedly told him all about her mom's new house and the barn and how nicely everything was coming along.

"That sounds great, I'm so happy for you girls. I'll have to plan a trip soon, but for now I have to run kiddo. Talk to you later!"

"Bye Dad. Love you!"

He'd already hung up. Darn it. That was alright, hopefully he would visit soon. That would be great.

Jade was upset when her parents got divorced – perhaps the most upset. They didn't get to see a lot of him growing up, and she was worried that with the divorce, they would see even less of him. But it actually wasn't that different. Jade was lucky that she was away at school at the time, and then she got married. Brandon reminded her a lot of her dad – it was partially the reason why she was so good at dealing with Brandon's moods. Jade took after her mom, and her mom always knew how to handle a pouter.

She went back into the kitchen and helped lay out some of the linens. She watched Morgan carefully, trying to absorb some information about how to iron. She hated ironing, and every time she tried it, she ended up with burnt or wet laundry. This was good for her, and it gave her a chance to talk to Morgan about less heavy topics.

About an hour later, her mom got a phone call and rushed off into a bedroom. She was back after about ten minutes and returned looking a bit stunned.

"What's going on? Did something happen?" asked Jade.

"No, nothing's wrong. I just got a call from Tammy."

"That's my dad's girlfriend," Jade told Morgan. Morgan nodded and kept ironing the tablecloth.

"She said that she overheard how well everything was going with the barn, and apparently she and Dad would love to plan a visit."

"That's great!" said Jade. "I'll be honest, I *did* talk it up to try to convince him."

Her mom nodded. "Also...she asked if we could have a surprise birthday party for your dad at the barn."

"But that's only a few weeks away," said Jade.

"I know." Her mom frowned. "But how could I say no?"

Morgan chimed in. "As my mom always used to say, 'No' is a full sentence!"

Jade laughed. "My mom can't say no. That's where I get it from."

Her mom clasped her hands together. "Oh come on, it'll be fun! Your dad will come out, and hopefully your brother and your sister too. It'll be really nice."

"Well I guess this means I should extend my visit for a bit longer to help out with everything," Morgan said quietly.

"No, you don't have to keep working here for free," her mom replied.

"I was actually hoping that there would be more for me to do. I'm not ready to go home yet."

Jade felt her heart swell and she quickly caught eyes with her mom.

"We certainly wouldn't kick you out," said Jade.

"Yes," her mom added. "I will take all the help that I can get!"

"Then I'm happy to stay," said Morgan, spreading out the tablecloth, a wide grin on her face.

Chapter 9

It was only a week, but Hank was successful in keeping his mind occupied and away from Saltwater Cove. Meeting Morgan Allen refocused him – he went back to the sheriff's office and spoke to every deputy involved with the Kelly Allen case. He looked through all of the information that they had and was able to confirm what he feared was true – they reached a dead end. They were unable to find the car, and neither Brock nor his mechanic Frankie were talking.

Earlier in the week, Hank paid a visit to Frankie on the mainland. Frankie was less than cooperative – friendly at first, but he quickly stopped answering questions when it came to Brock.

"I've got nothing to say about him," he said. "I work on his cars sometimes. He has a lot of beautiful and expensive cars. End of story."

"He must be a pretty great client if you loaned him your personal car," replied Hank.

Frankie shook his head. "It's not a crime to loan out your car to someone."

"It is when they commit a crime using the car."

"We both know that he was acquitted of the DUI. So nothing happened. Like I said, end of story. If you've got nothing else to say, I've got to get back to work."

It was obvious that Frankie was trying to hide something, but Hank didn't know how to get him to talk. He wasn't going to give up, though. When he got back to work on Monday, he decided to pool everything he could about Frankie and his business.

Two hours into his investigation, Lola stopped by his desk. "Hey Chief, you got a visitor."

"Tell them I'm not here."

"Your car is parked outside, though."

"Tell them I died," he said without looking up.

"You shouldn't joke about that!" said a familiar voice.

Hank's eyes shot up. "Margie! Lola didn't tell me that it was you."

Lola was already making her way out of the room but responded in a flat tone. "I'm full of surprises."

Hank stood up. "Please, have a seat. Sorry about that – I had a guy come every day last week to try to convince me that his neighbor is a witch. I thought it was him again."

She smiled warmly. "Sounds like a nuisance. You don't have to explain yourself to me."

They both took a seat. Margie looked nice, as usual, but he was going to keep things professional. "So what can I help you with today?"

"Well, I don't want to take up too much of your time. I need a recommendation for an electrician and a contractor. It seems that the barn will need to be up and running sooner than expected."

She smelled pretty nice, too. What was that? Was it just perfume? Or was it some mixture of flowers and cookies and joy?

Hank nodded. "Absolutely. No problem. How are things coming along?"

"Pretty good so far. Morgan is staying with me – she's been a huge help."

He crossed his arms tightly. "I'm sorry about springing her on you like that. I meant to check in and see how things were going, but –"

"Everything's great!" Margie said. "Really. I'm happy to have her."

Wow. She couldn't be any nicer if she tried. "I'm glad to hear it."

"About Morgan...I actually have another favor to ask."

Hank leaned in. "What's up?"

"I feel strange asking this," she said in a hushed voice. "But is there any way that you can get a copy of Morgan's birth certificate?"

He frowned. "I could. But I would need to provide documentation as to why I am looking for her birth certificate."

"Oh."

"Why would you need that?"

Margie sighed. "Well, it's a long story. Basically, Morgan was raised by her mom and her stepdad. She never met her biological father, but I think I *may* know who he was. But I don't want to say anything without definite proof and...it's very complicated."

"I see," said Hank leaning forward. "Unfortunately, it'd be best if Morgan requested it herself. I'm sure she has a copy at home somewhere."

"I don't want to bother her with it unless I actually know who it is. Do you know what I mean?"

Hank nodded. "Sure. Seems sensitive."

"Well in that case," Margie stood with a sigh. "I won't take up any more of your time. I'll just take your recommendations for the electrician and contractor."

Hank ripped out a sheet of paper from his notebook and scrawled down three names. "No problem at all."

"Oh – and this is kind of a strange request, too, but do you know anyone who could chop up a big tree? There was a storm a few nights ago, and a huge branch fell by the barn. Luckily it didn't do any damage, but it's too big for me to move myself."

Without thinking, Hank replied. "Oh, I would love to help you with that. I've got a chainsaw at home, and I could come and chop it up in no time. You'd have some nice firewood once it dries out."

"Oh you don't have to do that! I don't want to be any more of a bother to you than I already am."

"Please, I'm pretty sure you're the only reason that Morgan hasn't gone back onto that guy's property and I didn't have to arrest her."

Margie laughed. "Yes, I'm trying to be a good influence on her."

"So really, I owe you. I'd be happy to do it. I could stop by tonight after work?"

"Well only if I can get you to stay for dinner," said Margie. "I'm making enchiladas."

Hank smiled. "Now you made me an offer that I can't refuse. That lasagna was honestly the best thing I've had to eat in a year."

She gently poked him in the shoulder. "Oh you stop it!"

Hank felt goosebumps erupt on his arms. "It's true."

"We'll be expecting you for dinner – is seven okay?"

"That's perfect. See you then."

After she left, Hank sat at his desk and pretended to stare at his computer screen. But really, his mind was with her. He'd been so good about focusing on work, but as soon as she showed up again, it was like he couldn't help himself. One minute he was working hard, and the next he volunteered to be her personal lumberjack.

Hank went straight home after work to change out of his uniform. He then stood in front of his closet and faced a question that he hadn't thought about in ages – what should he wear? Margie had never seen him in regular clothes before, and truth be told, most of his regular clothes weren't in the best condition.

He rummaged through a drawer filled with t-shirts. At the bottom was a soft gray shirt that his wife always liked. He pulled it out and ran his hand over the fabric – she said that it always felt soft on her skin. He'd wear it on the weekends when she would lay against his shoulder or on his chest as they watched TV.

He folded the shirt and carefully placed it back in the drawer. What was he doing? Why was he trying to look nice for another woman? This was ridiculous – it was too soon to feel this way. It was too soon to look forward to seeing someone else. It was too soon to be happy.

He shut the drawer and grabbed a black T-shirt that was laying on the floor. He wasn't trying to impress anybody here, he just needed to chop up a tree for a friend, and he couldn't remember how long that shirt was on the floor or how it got there. It was perfect.

When he got to Margie's place, he knocked on her front door and she answered right away.

"Want to show me where that tree is?"

"Of course!"

Hank followed her to the barn silently. Margie had an incredible view of the ocean from both the house and the barn. He lingered, watching the water only for a moment before getting to work. In half an hour, he had the tree chopped up and stacked into a neat pile. While he was working, he came up with the plan of skipping dinner.

It would've been perfect, except Margie wouldn't hear of it.

"No! Please, come in right now. I'm just putting the last finishing touches. I already have some chips and guacamole laid out."

Guacamole? Now that was hard to resist. What harm could a few chips do? He decided he'd have a few bites and then head out.

Three hours later, he was still sitting at the table, laughing and telling stories with Morgan and Margie. It took Morgan a bit to warm up to him, but when she did, she was quite clever. And Margie...well, Hank enjoyed even hearing the sound of her voice. And her laugh – she had a great laugh.

When he finally got back to his car that night, he could no longer pretend – it was impossible for him to avoid her. Since his wife Corinne passed away, the only time he felt happy was when he was around Margie. That was an impossible feeling to resist – *she* was impossible for him to resist.

He thought that he would never be interested in anyone again; no one could measure up to the love and the life he'd had with Corinne. But Margie wasn't in competition. She was warm smiles, and fresh cupcakes, and a fantastic laugh. Her gentle spirit reminded him of Corinne, who told him, many times towards the end, that she wanted him to find someone else, to be happy.

"We'll see," he'd tell her, knowing that would never happen.

But now, he wondered if Corinne hand picked Margie herself and sent her on that ferry.

Chapter 10

When Margie got back into the house after saying goodbye to Hank, Morgan already had most of the dishes cleared from the table.

"You don't have to do that," she said.

"It's the least I can do," said Morgan as she loaded the dishwasher.

"Gosh I missed having a dishwasher."

"You didn't have one in your old apartment?"

"No." Margie took a seat at the kitchen bar. "And it was a very small place, too. So I couldn't have a big drying rack. It was cramped."

Morgan finished rinsing the last dish. "Chief Hank seems pretty nice."

"He does," Margie said, keeping her tone even.

"I think he likes you," said Morgan with a smile.

"Don't be ridiculous!" Margie rushed off to the dining room to wipe down the table and fuss about the chairs.

He certainly didn't like her, he was just being nice. In fact, he was being *too* nice, because she'd been quite a nuisance since she arrived on the island. He must think that she was crazy, asking for birth certificates and questioning him about dead people.

It was surprising that gruff Chief Hank volunteered, without question, to cut up that branch. And then he showed up in that black t-shirt with a big chainsaw at his side...

Well.

Margie always liked a man in uniform and thought that he looked cute in his chief outfit, but this was something else. He looked very...masculine. Very lumberjack-ish. She found herself stealing glances out of the window to watch him work.

He was very skilled with the chainsaw, and that was impressive in itself. But she didn't realize until she saw him throwing huge hunks of wood around how strong he was! His biceps strained against those little black sleeves. It was positively hard to look away.

She almost laughed to herself, because Hank was exactly the kind of guy who would've made Jeff feel insecure. Jeff was a good-looking man, sure. But he was rather slender, and his hair started thinning in his late twenties, so he became more and more preoccupied with how he looked.

He spent money on expensive suits, went to fancy salons and even tried some products to keep his hair from falling out. None of it worked, so he focused on the nice clothes and the nice cars. He became jealous when another man, especially one who looked stronger and had better hair than he did, spoke to Margie in an even slightly flirtatious manner.

Margie was *not* a flirt, but she liked to be nice to everyone she met. When men were nice back, though, it bothered Jeff. So Margie avoided talking to anyone that might probe Jeff's insecurities.

A smile tugged at the sides of her lips. Yes, Hank was definitely the kind of man that would annoy her ex-husband. Yet for years, she'd taken great strides to avoid being petty or bitter after the divorce, because she never wanted her kids to have a bad image of their father. She wasn't going to start with bad thoughts now! She decided that she better stop giggling to herself about Hank's muscles and instead focus on something productive.

Morgan didn't say anything else about Hank, and they went their respective ways for the evening. The next day, Margie was busy running errands. Jade planned to stay for the weekend again; she volunteered to set up a website for Saltwater Cove. Morgan volunteered to take some pictures – apparently, she had a nice camera and a passion for photography. It all seemed like it was coming together in a wonderful way.

The week flew by and Jade arrived early on Friday morning.

"This job of yours is so flexible!" said Margie when she picked her up at the ferry terminal. "It's great!"

"I know. It makes me nervous they like me so much."

"Oh Jade, when will you realize that you really *are* as wonderful as we all think you are?"

Jade smiled but said nothing.

Margie decided to drop it. She was glad that she could see Jade more often now and that she could balance out Brandon's constant nagging and nitpicking.

When they got back to the house, Jade got to work right away on building the website, and Margie worked with

Morgan to set up the barn to make it look like a wedding was about to occur.

"I think weddings are going to be your big moneymaker," commented Morgan. "But I'm sure that you can do graduation parties, birthday parties, retirement parties..."

"That's a lot of partying," said Margie with a laugh.

"If it's for a wedding though, you can charge double for everything. They won't notice."

"I would never do that! I just want to make a living, I don't need to make a fortune."

"Suit yourself!"

They set up the tables, chairs, table cloths, and even some simple centerpieces; they wanted to get a few pictures of the barn looking its best. They had to entirely avoid the bathroom area, though, because the contractor that Margie hired didn't stop by that week at all like he promised he would. Margie called him a few times and he didn't answer. She didn't want to get worried without reason, but it didn't seem like a good sign.

Morgan had the idea to string up some bistro lights to give a soft, romantic look. It took both of them over an hour, climbing up ladders and sweating, to get the lights into place.

"That was a lot harder than I expected," said Morgan.

Margie nodded. "Me too. But it does look incredible."

"Have you figured out the catering yet?"

"Well, nothing is finalized, but I've talked to the owners of three different restaurants on the island, and all of them were interested in putting together catering menus and prices."

"That's amazing!"

Margie bent over and plugged in the end of the string of bistro lights. Luckily, they all lit up. "Thank you. What was amazing is that they let me try some of their dishes, and every-thing was wonderful. And doesn't that just look lovely?"

"I really out did myself," said Morgan with a laugh.

"How about we go inside and have a drink before we do the rest of this?" said Margie.

"That's a good idea."

They went back into the house and Margie was excited to see Jade's progress. To her surprise, Jade was in the kitchen chatting with Chief Hank.

"Oh! Hank! It's nice to see you."

"It's nice to see you too Margie. And you, Morgan."

"What's up?"

He was wearing a t-shirt again. He didn't have the chainsaw with him, but he still managed to look big and strong.

"Not too much, I wanted to stop by and see how things were going. I have the weekend off and...well, I have a boat."

Margie nodded slowly. "That's nice."

He laughed and kept talking. "Well, what I mean is, I was planning on taking the boat out tomorrow. Normally, Mike would go out with me, but seeing that you ran him out of town and stole his house, I was thinking that maybe – you'd want to go out with me?"

Chapter 11

Jade felt her eyes bulge and had to remind herself to look natural. Was Chief Hank asking her mom out on a date?

"Me? Go out with you?" her mom said.

"Yeah, on the boat. Have you had a chance to go on the water at all – other than the ferry?"

"No, I can't say that I have."

Morgan chimed in. "Oh, do you think that you'll see killer whales? Or do you call them orcas?"

"You can call them whatever you like," said Hank. "It's a little early in the season to see the resident orcas. But you never know when you might see the transients."

"What's the difference?" Morgan leaned onto the kitchen bar, resting her chin on her hand.

"The resident orcas are the ones that only eat salmon. They tend to follow the salmon, and often they're only here during the summer time. They're the group at risk of extinction."

"Is that because of all the boats or something?" asked Jade.

Hank shook his head. "There are a lot of theories, of course. But the biggest thing that we've seen is that some of the whales are starving. One of the main rivers for the salmon has a bunch of dams on it, which causes problems for the salmon spawning, and then you have the problem of overfishing, and the end result is that the whales don't have any salmon to eat. And they starve to death."

Her mom gasped. "That's awful! I had no idea it was so bad."

"Every year we have little victories where we're able to do something good for the whales. If we're lucky, the residents should come back in July or so."

"What about the other ones?" asked Morgan.

"The transient orcas only eat mammals. Porpoises, seals, sea lions. There's *plenty* for them to eat. But they come and go much more randomly. You never know when you're going to see them."

"So you *have* seen them before? Out on your boat?" asked her mom.

"Oh yeah! All the time. It's really amazing."

Morgan sat up, a wide smile on her face. "Sounds like a lovely time."

Jade's eyes darted between the three of them. Was she missing something? Was Hank over here all the time hitting on her mom or something? That didn't seem very...professional of him!

"Oh I don't know, there is so much to do around here."

Morgan waved a hand. "I'll be here all day and I can work on whatever you need. You should go! And Chief Hank, you have to promise to take me out on the boat sometime. Maybe when the whales are here."

"You got it kid."

Jade looked at her mom. Her cheeks were flushed – something that the other two may not notice, but she knew that response quite well. Did her mom *like* this guy? It made sense – sort of. They were around the same age, and it seemed like he was nice to her. It just seemed so odd. Her mom never dated after the divorce, she never even mentioned it. Jade assumed that she didn't want to meet anyone else.

Maybe she was wrong. Her dad already had a few girlfriends since the divorce. Jade used to hope that they would get back together, but that seemed unlikely. Maybe her mom wanted to have a boyfriend. Maybe she was lonely.

The thought made her sad. Why *shouldn't* her mom get to go on a boat date?

"Yeah mom," Jade added. "You should definitely go."

Their eyes met and Jade smiled.

"It does sound like a very nice time," her mom said slowly. "I can pack a picnic!"

"That would be great."

Jade watched Hank carefully. It seemed like he had actually been holding his breath until her mom agreed to go with him. That was kind of sweet.

He had *better* be a nice guy, or Jade would...she didn't know what she would do, but it would be bad. Her mom deserved the best.

"So Morgan," Jade said, "let me show you how I have the website set up so far."

"Oh, *good idea*."

Jade had to force herself not to burst into laughter at that moment; Morgan was a bit heavy handed, plus she was giving her a funny look. Luckily, they managed to leave the room before doing anything obvious, a smile pulling on Jade's lips.

Chapter 12

It'd been years – *years* – since Margie went out on a date. Jeff wasn't a romantic guy, but whenever he threw a party for the business or needed to host a client, he would take her out to a really nice dinner or even a show. Margie tried to think of the last time they'd gone out like that, but she sincerely couldn't remember.

Even still, this was different. This wasn't really going out on a date. Hank just wanted her to see the water – to see his boat, apparently. She did find it odd that he hadn't invited Jade or Morgan on the boat as well.

What if they wanted to come and see the whales? When she brought it up to them after he left, they were both adamant that they had no interest in going.

"I have a lot to do before I catch the ferry tomorrow," said Jade.

"And I need to edit all of these photos to get them ready for the website," said Morgan. "There's absolutely no way that either of us could go boating tomorrow. But you should! You need to have some fun every once in a while."

"Yeah Mom. The weather is supposed to be great. You'll have fun," added Jade.

Margie did feel better that Jade didn't seem against the whole idea. She wouldn't want Jade to feel strange about her spending time with a man other than her father. Yes, they were divorced, but she knew how uncomfortable it made her kids – especially the girls – whenever Jeff brought around one of his girlfriends.

Margie didn't want to do that to them. She was perfectly content with her life as it was. Her children were her focus, and she was just now getting a chance to bring them all together again. She wouldn't risk it on a romance with some guy, no matter how good he looked in his sheriff's uniform.

Or chopping wood.

Okay, no need to keep bringing up that image!

Also, no one made a comment that it was actually a date, so Margie felt okay going. Hank was, for the time being, her only friend on the island. Soon, Morgan would have to go back home and Margie would have no one to hang out with.

Well, she had Jade of course, and so far she'd been lucky in spending a lot of time with her, but that couldn't last forever. Brandon was sure to be annoyed that Jade spent so much time on the island. Margie hoped that eventually she'd get to know some other people on the island; surely there was a book club or quilting club that she could join. Once her business was off the ground, she would investigate that further. For now, she was happy to have Hank as her friend.

As promised, she packed a nice picnic for the trip. She didn't have a picnic basket, but she decided that an insulated bag that she usually used for grocery shopping would do. It wasn't cute, but it did the job. She packed sandwiches with ice packs, freshly cut fruit, some fancy cheese, and cherry tomatoes. She put some soda in there too, but she didn't know what Hank even liked. For good measure, she baked a batch of brownies as well.

He told her that he would pick her up at eleven on Sunday morning, and true to his word, he arrived promptly at eleven o'clock. Margie took one last look at herself in the mirror before she went to meet him – she'd decided to wear a pair of olive khakis with her bright yellow rain jacket. She also had a pair of boat shoes that she hadn't worn in ages, and it felt like the perfect occasion to bring them out again. She leaned forward and made sure that she didn't have anything stuck in her teeth before heading out the door.

"Good morning!" said Hank as he got out of his truck.

"Hi! I hope you're ready for a big picnic."

"Always," he said as he ran around the side of his truck to open the door for her.

Margie rushed over, hoping that neither Jade nor Morgan were watching from the house. She decided not to look at the windows to check.

She settled into her seat and Hank rolled down the driveway.

"This is a nice truck," she commented.

"Thanks."

They kept driving. Margie didn't know what else to say, but she hated feeling awkward.

"Do we need to go and pick up the boat?"

Hank shook his head. "No, I keep it docked year round. The dock is actually not too far from here."

"Oh. That's nice."

They rode the rest of the way in silence. Why was he being so quiet? Why was *she* being so quiet? Maybe this really *was* a date. Maybe she shouldn't have worn this outfit...she even brought a goofy hat to block the sun. It wasn't a very date-like item to bring.

They reached the dock and Hank parked the truck. Margie could see several boats bobbing peacefully in the water, glistening in the sun.

"Which one is yours?"

"The red one." He extended an arm to point it out.

As they approached it, Margie squinted to see the name on the back. "The Cori Express?"

"Yeah," Hank said, rubbing the back of his head. "It was kind of a joke. For my wife – Corinne. When I got the boat, I convinced her that I could use it to shuttle her between the islands whenever she wanted."

Oh. He had a wife. So this most certainly *wasn't* a date. Margie was surprised that she felt bothered by this. "That was nice of you."

He laughed. "She didn't think it was funny. But it ended up being helpful when she was sick. We had to go to the mainland for a lot of her doctor's appointments and treatments, and sometimes the ferry schedule just didn't work for her."

"Oh," replied Margie, her voice falling. "May I ask what she was sick with?"

"Cancer. It was, ah, kidney cancer. It spread before we even knew it was there. She passed away almost two years ago."

"I'm so sorry. Do you have any other family on the island?"

Hank hopped onto the boat and extended a hand to help Margie. She accepted.

"No, unfortunately not," he said with a chuckle. "My kids fled to the opposite ends of the world after my wife died."

"What do you mean?"

"Well my oldest, my son Jacob, he moved to Australia."

"Oh my! How exciting."

"Yeah, he loves it. I've been to visit twice, it's an amazing country. And my daughter Amanda – she moved to London. She works in marketing, and when her company gave her the option to go, she took it."

Without thinking, Margie commented, "It must be very lonely." She paused, realizing her mistake, and said, "I mean –"

Hank laughed. "No, it's okay. It is. I know it's hard for the kids to come back here, but I miss them. Yet somehow, I just can't bring myself to leave."

"Well I think it's wonderful that you have a place for them to call home – even if they're not quite ready to come back yet."

"I never thought of it that way," said Hank as he untied the boat. "You can put a positive spin on anything, can't you?"

Margie laughed. "I try. That's what I'm trying to do for my kids now. I just want to have a place that we can all be together and be happy."

"I think you've achieved that. Are they coming for Christmas?"

"Well hopefully sooner. My ex-husband's girlfriend suggested that we throw him a surprise birthday party here in a few weeks. At the barn, I mean. That's why I'm in such a rush to get everything done. And as of right now, I think that all of the kids can make it."

"That's great. My daughter is coming to visit next week actually. It's the – well, it's the two-year anniversary of my wife passing away. But we try not to focus on that date. She's really coming to celebrate her mom's birthday."

"That's nice that she can make it here."

"It is. My son can't, but we're going to video call him. I'll visit him soon. Sorry to talk so much about my depressing life," he said rubbing his face. "I'm just not used to talking to anyone really."

Margie smiled. "You don't have to apologize to me. And your life isn't depressing. It's...very normal, actually."

He smiled and started the boat. Margie took a seat. It was too bad that he felt that way – she really didn't mind hearing about his past, even if it was sad. It was actually quite nice to get to know him. So far, it seemed like she was the only one sharing information – bits and pieces of her life that made her seem a little crazy. It was nice to know that he was human too. Plus, the more she knew about him, the more relaxed she felt, and of course, the more she liked him.

He took the boat south, down the west side of the island. They rode past the Lime Kiln Lighthouse, and he stopped his boat there for a while.

"Later in the summer, the resident killer whales will swim up and down this side of the island, just hunting salmon. You can stand at the lighthouse and watch them. It's just incredible."

"Do you think that we'll see any today?"

Hank frowned. "I don't know. I haven't heard of any sightings unfortunately."

"Then we'll just have to come out again," said Margie.

He smiled broadly. "Good, so I must not have bored you too much if you're willing to come out again."

"Of course not! This is great."

They continued around the south tip of the island all the way to Cattle Point. He peppered in some interesting history about the islands. They were extremely lucky in their non-whale wildlife watching. Past Cattle Point, they came upon what looked like a huge flock of bald eagles. There had to be at least ten or twelve of them just spreading their wings over the bluffs, letting the sea breeze keep them afloat. Margie tried to take a picture with her cell phone, but they were too far away.

"I should have Morgan bring her fancy camera," she said.

"Oh that's right. I'll bring her out on the boat too, some other time." He cleared his throat rather loudly. "But I'm glad that you agreed to come with me. I...really enjoy spending time with you."

Margie turned to him – his cheeks looked slightly red. Was it the sun? No – it couldn't be. He certainly wasn't a man who was used to sharing his feelings, but it seemed that he was trying. Margie had no problem sharing her feelings most of the time.

She reached out and touched his arm. "That's good Hank, because I like spending time with you, too."

They continued around the island and spotted porpoises, harbor seals, and countless sea lions sunbathing on the rocks. As wonderful of a time as she was having, Margie was starting to get hungry. She suggested that they find a shaded area and settle in for their picnic. Hank was happy to oblige, and he directed the boat as close to the shore as was safe so they could catch some shade from the trees.

"Now it's not much, and I didn't know what you liked, but I packed a couple of things..."

"This is incredible!" he said, looking at the sandwiches and the cheese. "Everything you make is incredible. I knew that I should've smuggled a bottle of wine on board."

Now Margie felt her own cheeks turning red. She wasn't used to that sort of praise. Was he trying to manipulate her? No – he didn't seem like the type.

"That's enough out of you. And we couldn't have wine, you can't drink and drive a boat!"

"I'm a pretty big guy. I could handle one glass. If I'd known you were going to put together something so fancy –"

"Here, stop calling a simple picnic fancy and have a sandwich." She thrust one into his hand. "And when was the last time you had some fresh tomatoes?"

He shrugged. "Does pizza count?"

"No, pizza does not count."

They laughed, both catching the same giddiness; Margie wasn't sure if it came from the excitement of seeing all the animals, the beautiful weather or the fact that if this was a first date, it was going amazingly.

They finished off the picnic, with Hank eating half of the brownies, again full of praise, and headed back to dock the boat. Margie was having a marvelous time, but she wanted to get back to the house and get some things in order. He drove her home, and unlike the trip out to the boat, they talked the entire time.

She worried that the girls might be watching from the window and was afraid that he might try to hug her or something – so as soon as he stopped the truck, she opened the door and hopped out.

"Thank you for the lovely day! We'll have to do it again."

"No, thank you. This was the most fun I've had in ages."

She smiled. "Take care!"

Margie turned and walked to the front door, ignoring the two sets of eyes peering at her from the front window.

Chapter 13

As soon as Margie pushed the door open, there was a flurry of activity inside the house.

"Hello girls," she called out. "Were you doing some bird watching from the window?"

Jade and Morgan appeared in the hallway.

"No, we just heard a car pull up and..." Jade's voice trailed off.

"We wanted to see if Chief was going to kiss you," added Morgan.

Jade's hand darted to her mouth. Margie tried to think of something stern to say back, but nothing came to her. To her surprise, it wasn't the *worst* thing in the world to have a man interested in her. Especially someone as nice as Hank.

Morgan crossed her arms. "But we were *sorely* disappointed."

"Morgan!" Jade groaned.

The whole exchange made Margie laugh. "Well I'm sorry to disappoint you girls, but this isn't *The Bachelor*!"

"So he *didn't* give you a rose?" asked Morgan.

Margie shook her head. "No, he did not."

"So," Jade said, clearing her throat. "How was the boat? Did you see any orcas?"

"No, we didn't. But we saw lots of other animals! Bald eagles, sea lions, harbor seals...it was really nice. And Hank said that he would love to take you two out on the boat sometime."

Morgan frowned. "Isn't he a little old for us?"

Now Jade started laughing. "You're *ridiculous*."

"I know," Morgan said with a smile.

Luckily that was all of the teasing that Margie had to endure for her sort of, kind of date. For the rest of the evening, Morgan excitedly showed her some of the pictures that she'd taken and edited, and Jade showed her the beginnings of the website. It wasn't completely done because Jade ran into a few setbacks, but she really wanted to get the website up and running, so she asked her boss if she could work remotely for the day. That way she didn't have to take the ferry back until Monday evening.

Margie loved having them both in the house, though she did worry that Brandon might start to complain that Jade was over too much. She kept it to herself – for now. She knew that her kids' relationships were their own business, but it was hard to keep quiet sometimes.

On Tuesday that week, Margie made another trip to the mainland to buy some basics for the other bedrooms in the house. She wanted the kids to be comfortable when they visited, to relax and feel at home; and even if the barn might not be ready for the party, she could at least have the home ready for her family.

At the very least, she wanted each room to have a bed frame, a mattress, and a nightstand. Hank was gracious enough to loan her his truck so she could easily fit a number of items. He offered to come and help as well, but she declined – she was perfectly able to make the trip with her furniture buddy Morgan. They drove down to the Seattle Ikea and had a field day – Margie ended up with matching dressers for the bedrooms as well. The prices were great and the furniture looked cute, too.

Hank stopped by on Wednesday and insisted on helping her build the furniture. Since it was all from Ikea, there was a lot of work to be done, but she hated to ask him any more favors.

"I'm sure you've got lots of other important things to do," she told him.

He leaned over and peered into the doorway of the first bedroom, where the entire floor was covered in cardboard boxes along with bits and pieces of furniture. "I can promise you that I don't have anything important to do. I feel like you could use some help with this. Don't the instructions say that this is a two-person job?"

Margie bit her lip and cast a look at the paper instructions, splayed open on the floor. "It *does* have a picture of two people in the beginning. Well, they weren't exactly people. They didn't have faces or anything."

He laughed. "But they have four hands between them?"

She nodded. "They definitely have four hands."

"Then it sounds like you're two hands short."

"You've got me there." Margie laughed. If the man insisted on building furniture with her, then what was she supposed to do? Send him away?

They got to work and spent the next two hours putting together one bed, one dresser and one night stand. Margie couldn't believe how long it took. Hank was handy though, and despite mentioning several times that he had a drill back home that would make things easier, they just kept tackling each piece as a team and taking their time. Hank was sure that they would be Ikea experts by the end.

Margie didn't mind that they didn't have a tool to speed things up; she quite enjoyed passing the hours with him. He had great stories about living on the island and being a deputy. The only issue was that once they finished the furniture for one room, her entire body hurt. The thought of doing it all over again for the other bedroom, even with their new expertise, was painful.

"Oof!" she said out loud as she stood up, hips popping.

"What's up?" asked Hank.

"I forgot that Morgan told me that I could use her yoga mat while building this stuff."

"Oh okay. Where is Morgan today?"

"She wanted to go for a hike and take some pictures," Margie replied, stretching out her back. Everything was sore. Maybe it wasn't a good idea to do the other room. Yet she was having so much fun...

Hank grunted. "A hike. Sure. She told me that's what she was doing when she trespassed on Brock's property."

"Well hopefully she's not doing that again. You have to let kids make their own mistakes!" Margie added with a laugh. "I'm going to go and get the yoga mat. I think she said she keeps it under the bed."

Margie went to Morgan's room and got on her hands and knees to look under the bed. The room was nearly pitch black because of the light blocking curtains that Morgan hung up.

Squinting, she could just make out the outline of what looked like a yoga mat. She stuck her hand under the bed and pulled it out. Unfortunately, she was a bit too forceful and she also pulled something else out with it: a small shoebox with a loose lid, and the contents immediately spilled onto the floor.

"Oh for goodness sake," Margie muttered. She stood up and turned on the light so she could see what she was doing. When she got back on the floor to clean up the mess she made, she saw that the shoebox was full of trinkets and pictures.

It was quite sweet – Morgan collected postcards, rocks from the beach, even a sprig of dry lavender. All mementos from the island. There was also a stack of pictures with land-scapes and wildlife. Margie knew that she shouldn't look through them without asking, but they were so beautiful, and the picture sitting on top was a gorgeous shot of the barn at sunset. Margie sat on the floor and slowly sifted through the photos.

She was staring at a picture of the coast, trying to figure out where it was taken, when a small photograph fell to the floor. She reached down and grabbed it, turning it right side up.

What she saw made her stomach drop. It was a picture of Jeff and Kelly – just two squares cut out from what looked like a photo booth strip. In the top picture they were smiling – Kelly was exactly as Margie remembered her. Bright eyes, long dark hair. In the second picture, they were kissing deeply.

Margie's hand started shaking. She dropped the rest of the photos, needing both hands to keep steady. How could it be? How could her husband have hidden this from her? How could he have done something like this – not just to Margie. Not just to Kelly. But to the kids...was her whole life with him a lie?

And Morgan. Sweet Morgan. What was Margie going to say to her?

What on *earth* was she going to do?

Chapter 14

It'd been a few minutes and Margie still hadn't come back with that yoga mat. Maybe she couldn't find it? Hank was having a great time hanging out with her, but he agreed that being down on the ground for so long wasn't good for anyone's joints.

"Margie?" He made his way towards Morgan's room. "I have an idea. Maybe we could at least make the dresser and the nightstand on the kitchen table, and –"

"Oh, I don't know," she said quickly. "I'm in...worse shape than I realized. Once I stood up, everything was...you know."

"Are you okay?"

"Yeah, I'm fine, I just...I think I need to take a break for the rest of the night."

Darn. He didn't want to go home yet. "Okay. Well, would you like to grab some dinner in town or something?"

"That's very sweet of you, but I really just don't feel well. It came on all of a sudden."

She did look a little pale. "I can run and get you some chicken soup if you like? I'm not a good enough cook to make my own, unfortunately. But there is a shop not too far from my place that makes great soup."

She smiled and shook her head. "No, that's very sweet of you, but that's okay. I think...I'm so sorry, but I just need to lie down."

"Okay, no problem. Sorry that you don't feel well. I can come back later this week to help you finish the furniture. My daughter is coming on Friday, so I'll be a bit busy, but I'm sure she doesn't want to spend all of her time with me. And I would love for you to meet her."

Margie didn't respond; she seemed to be staring off into the distance.

Hank leaned down to get onto her level. "You sure you're okay?"

She startled and looked back at him. "Yes, I'm fine. I think I must have caught something."

"Okay, well then, I'll get out of your hair. Let me know when you need more help with this, I'm happy to come back. I can bring that drill."

"Thanks Hank. I appreciate it."

He hated leaving her when she didn't feel well, but it was clearly what she wanted. He gathered up his things, said goodbye, and headed out the front door. The rest of the night, he sat in front of the TV and watched some reruns of Seinfeld.

Hank had to go into work on Thursday, and once his shift was done he stopped by to check in on Margie. Unfortunately, she wasn't home, and he wondered if it was weird for him to drop by like that. He decided that maybe he should announce himself in the future, and for now just send Margie a text message to see how she was doing.

Hank had some errands to run that night to distract him, and to his surprise, Margie answered his message quickly. He wondered if she was also used to texting because of her daughters.

"I'm doing okay, thanks for asking. Still not 100%. And for the life of me I can't get the contractor to get here and finish up these bathrooms. He's driving me nuts!"

Hank frowned. "Who did you hire again?"

"Eddie Mills. I'm starting to wonder if he gave me the runaround."

"I'll have a talk with him," replied Hank.

He hadn't recommended Eddie, but he remembered Margie telling him that the guys that he told her about were busy. Eddie had a tepid reputation on the island. He did good work, but he was known to take advantage of people when it suited him. He thought he was a tough guy – and he liked to brag about the things he could get away with.

Hank felt his blood pressure rise just thinking about Eddie stringing Margie along. It wasn't that Margie needed to be protected – she was perfectly capable of taking care of herself. But Eddie, in his endless pursuit of proving how macho of a man he was, thought it was funny to mess around with people who didn't know how long a job should take.

"Women," he once said, rolling his eyes, "are my *best* customers. I can tell 'em I'm looking for a special wrench for weeks. They have no idea."

Hank promptly told him that his customers were probably just being polite and thought he had some sort of problem. Eddie didn't like that. He was *not* Hank's kind of guy, and Hank felt the irresistible urge to protect Margie from Eddie's crude ways.

On Friday morning, he was pretty pleased with how clean he got the house. It took a couple of days to get to a decent level, but now he felt that he could maintain it going forward.

Before that, it seemed like there was no point. Truth be told, he now found himself wondering, "What if Margie wants to stop by sometime?" She might think that he was filthy! Plus his daughter liked a clean house.

Amanda came in on the early afternoon ferry. She flew into Seattle the evening before and stayed in the city with one of her friends for the night. It made the journey a bit easier for her, especially with the jet lag.

She then rented a car and drove up to Anacortes. Hank imagined a fun moment when he could stand at the ferry terminal waiting for her with a bouquet of flowers, but since she drove herself, he instead waited at the house with a bouquet of flowers.

When he heard the door open, he jumped up with the excitement of a dog who hadn't seen its owner in years. "Amanda!"

"Dad!"

He hugged her and picked her up off the ground. "I've missed you. How was your trip?"

"I've missed you too Dad. Put me down!"

He laughed and set her back on the ground. She was built like her mother – petite and delicate – but she did inherit his eyes.

He handed her the bouquet of roses. "These are for you."

She laughed. "Thanks Dad. I'll put them back on the table. Very nice."

"You know," he crossed his arms, "I don't just keep flowers around here for anybody."

She nodded. "I got that feeling about you. Oh! I got something for you too."

"Oh yeah? I told you not to waste your money on your old man."

She turned around, unzipped the pocket on her bag, and pulled out a container. "This is *bacon* flavored tea."

He reached out and unscrewed the lid, taking a whiff. "Wow. That really smells like bacon."

Amanda clapped her hands together. "I knew you'd love it."

"Have you tried it yet?"

"No, it looks disgusting."

They both laughed. Hank put on some water and they settled onto the couch to chat. Amanda had about a thousand things to tell him, which was nice. He liked sitting catching up on what was new with her.

Normally, she called him at least once a week, but it was much easier in person to assess how she was doing. She seemed cheerful – she was full of smiles and she had funny stories about her job and her friends. She loved living in London, minus a few annoyances.

"It sounds like San Juan has lost you forever," said Hank.

Amanda sighed. "Oh come on Dad. I might still move back – someday. I just...moved to a bigger island."

He laughed. "I'm just happy that you're happy."

"What's new with you? What's new on the island?"

Margie's face flashed in his mind, but for some reason, the only thing he could say was, "Nothing. Nothing at all."

"Typical. Nothing ever happens here."

"Actually..." He took a sip of the bacon tea. It wasn't great – but he didn't hate it, which was slightly odd. "I've been putting some extra time into that case. You know the one I told you about? That lady who was hit with the car."

"The one who died?"

"Yeah. Her daughter showed up on the island looking for clues. Really made me take a fine toothed comb over all the evidence we have."

Amanda nodded. "Did you find anything?"

"Not really. But I'm going to keep looking."

"Ah. Okay. Any orca sightings yet?"

"Unfortunately not. We can go on the boat later this week and look for them."

"Sounds good."

"Are you hungry? I was thinking we can get dinner in town later. Whatever you like."

"I would *love* some tacos." Amanda stood up and straightened her blouse. "There is no good Mexican food in London, I swear."

Hank laughed. "Perfect. Oh actually – do you mind if we stop at one place on the way?"

"Fine with me."

They got into the truck and Hank drove towards Friday Harbor. Eddie lived just outside of town, so Hank thought it might be a good idea to pay him a little visit. When they got to the house, he asked Amanda to stay in the car before going to the front door and knocking. Eddie opened the door right away.

"Hey Hank, good to see you man. Do you want to come in for a beer?"

He shook his head. "No Eddie. I'm here as a favor for a friend."

"Oh yeah? Am I in some sort of trouble?" Eddie said with a laugh.

"That depends. Do you ever plan on finishing the job that Margie Clifton paid you for?"

Eddie took a small step back and put his hands up. "Whoa whoa, I don't know what she told you –"

"She didn't tell me anything. I've been helping her around the barn, and every time I stop by, I can tell you haven't even touched those bathrooms. What's the matter, been too busy?"

"No, I was actually going to go there on Wednesday."

Hank narrowed his eyes. "Wednesday?"

"I meant Monday! Yeah, first thing Monday morning."

Hank smiled and placed a hand on Eddie's shoulder. "That's great to hear Eddie. Well, I've got to run, but you enjoy the rest of your evening."

Eddie nodded quickly. "You too Chief."

Hank turned and walked back to his truck. He tried taking some deep breaths. He really didn't like that guy, but at least it seemed like he was able to get through to him.

"What was that about?" asked Amanda when he got back in the truck.

He shrugged. "Nothing really. Eddie was just stringing along a friend of mine."

"Margie, you said? I've never heard of her," said Amanda slowly. "Is she new to the island?"

He turned around to back out of the driveway. "Uh, yeah. Kind of new. You 'member Mike? It's his sister. He sold her his property."

"Oh, okay."

He thought about telling her more about Margie, but she wasn't asking any more questions. And he felt strange talking about Margie. He put on some music and they got to the restaurant a few minutes later.

It wasn't until after they put their order in for tacos that Amanda started again. "So that's where you were the other day? When I called?"

"Messing with Eddie?" Hank said with a laugh.

"No, with that lady. What's her name."

He tried to keep his tone casual. "Margie."

"Yeah. Margie."

Hank could sense the shift in her mood. Normally, she'd be cheerful any time that there were tacos nearby, but she didn't seem excited now. She wasn't going to let this go. Hank decided it might be best to skim over some of the details.

"Well, actually –"

"Chief Hank? Is that you?" said a familiar voice behind him.

Hank turned around. Morgan and Margie stood in the entrance of the restaurant.

Oh boy. How could their timing be *so* impossibly bad?

"Hi Hank!" said Margie, walking towards them.

Hank felt like a trapped animal. He looked at his daughter, then back at Margie. "Oh, hey Margie, how's it going?"

Play it cool. Like Margie is just a friend. Well – they *were* just friends. That should be easy to act that way then, right?

"It looks like Chief is with a younger woman," said Morgan in a fake whisper.

Not a good joke right now Morgan. Hank stood up. "Guys, this is my daughter Amanda. Amanda, this is Margie, and Morgan."

Amanda stood up and shook both of their hands. "It's nice to meet you."

"It's nice to meet you too."

He stood there for a second. It was not as easy to act natural as he'd hoped. He had no idea what to say, so finally he blurted out, "Tacos huh? Good stuff."

Margie nodded. "Yeah, Morgan convinced me to come here to get dinner."

"When are you coming to build the rest of the furniture Chief?" asked Morgan.

Amanda looked at him; Hank could feel her glare and avoided it.

"You know, whenever you need me," he said. "I have that drill that would help. That I told you about."

"I'd really like to decorate in there," said Morgan.

Margie hushed her. "Well then, you can build everything yourself, don't bother him. Hank is busy. We'll let you two get back to your meal. We just ordered some takeout, and I'm guessing it's the bag sitting there on the counter."

"Okay, it was nice seeing you. Enjoy your food."

"You too!"

They picked up their food and in less than two minutes, they were gone. In the meantime, Hank and Amanda's food arrived.

Amanda leaned forward. "What was *that* all about Dad?"

"I don't know what you mean," he answered right away.

Never answer right away.

Amanda sat back and crossed her arms. "That lady. Are you guys...dating or something?"

"No! Not at all. We're just – friends. She's new on the island, and I'm trying to make her feel welcome, and I'm helping her out a little bit. She is Mike's sister, so I feel like I really need to help her."

"And that girl? Is that her daughter?"

"Oh. Morgan? No. She's actually the daughter of that lady who passed away."

"Oh." Amanda took a bite of her taco and chewed slowly.

Hank stuffed most of a taco into his mouth. Amanda was onto him. She was more worldly than other young women her age – she never would've been caught snooping around Brock's place like Morgan was. She was extremely successful, which he was proud of – of course. But she knew when someone was lying, *especially* when he was lying.

"Because you know what?" she finally said. "I'd think it'd be *pretty* messed up if you started dating someone so soon after mom died."

There it was. He closed his eyes and rubbed his face. "We're not dating, Amanda. I wouldn't do that."

"Good. Because that would be ridiculous."

He softened his tone and reached out to grab her hand. "You have nothing to worry about. Okay?"

She crossed her arms. "Okay."

He cleared his throat and took a sip of water. It was time to change the subject. "So, do you want to go out on the boat tomorrow?"

Amanda picked a piece of lettuce out of her teeth. "Yeah. Fine."

He smiled. "Great."

They were able to finish their meal without any more issues. But Hank knew that Amanda was right – he'd felt the same way, but chose to ignore the feeling. It was too soon to date, even if it was someone as lovely as Margie. He would just have to...find a way to avoid her.

Yeah. From now on, no more Margie.

Chapter 15

They were hardly out of earshot from the restaurant when Morgan spoke again.

"Why was Chief being so weird? Did you guys have a fight or something?"

"No, of course not," Margie said, trying to keep her tone light. "He was probably just surprised to see us – you know, when he was with his daughter."

"*Oh,*" said Morgan. "Do you think he wasn't ready for you to, like, meet her?"

Margie laughed. "No – I don't think – why are we even on this topic? More importantly, you can't just ask people to come over and build your furniture!"

Morgan shrugged. "I don't really want him to build the furniture, I just thought that you two had a nice time together, and..."

"Thank you for that. But that's not very polite."

They drove in silence. After a few minutes, Morgan responded. "I'm sorry. Sometimes I feel awkward I...overdo it. With the jokes."

"It's alright," Margie said with a smile. "I just – you know this is all very new for me. Spending time with a man."

"A *nice* man?"

Margie's heart jumped. Why did she say "nice" like *that*? Did Morgan know about Jeff? And that Jeff was *not* a nice man? Was she in on it this whole time?

"I don't know what you mean by that," Margie responded. "But yes, he's a very nice man."

"I just mean that your...never mind."

A Bonnie Tyler song came onto the radio and it was the perfect excuse for Margie to change the subject. "Oh! Do you hear that? Guess who!"

Morgan groaned but didn't make any complaints. Margie turned up the music so she could be alone with her thoughts.

Morgan wasn't wrong – Hank was acting strangely. Did he know about Jeff? Maybe he actually did look up the birth certificate and saw that it was her ex-husband's name as the father. But would he even know her husband's name? That didn't make much sense. But if it said "Jeff Clifton" he could obviously put it together.

Part of her hoped that Hank *did* know. At least she wouldn't be the only one with this secret. It'd only been a few days, but it felt like it was killing her. How had Jeff hidden this for so many years? Did he have no heart?

No – Margie told herself not to think that way. It was much too easy to become the bitter ex-wife. And that was not what she wanted for her family. They were only three weeks away from Jeff's surprise party, and they were expecting nearly sixty people. All of the kids were coming to the island and planning to stay for the week after the party. It was going to be lovely.

If Margie came in accusing Jeff of – she couldn't even think of the words. Having an illegitimate child? Cheating on her? Lying for all these years?

No, something wasn't right. It was hard to think about – hard to focus on. They got back to the house and enjoyed their dinner. It was Morgan's idea – she said that she stopped in there for lunch and thought that Margie would really like it. She was right – the tacos were delicious.

When they were cleaning up, Margie decided to broach an uncomfortable topic. "Have you told your dad yet that you've been staying here?"

"No, not yet. I've been calling him regularly, but I just know that if I tell him the truth he's going to want to know who I've been staying with, and then he may not believe me." She paused. "Hey! Why don't *you* talk to him for me?"

Margie's stomach dropped. What were the chances that her stepfather knew her name? Or that he remembered a Jeff Clifton from his wife's past?

"Oh, I don't think that's a good idea."

"Oh come on, please?"

"You are an adult young lady, and this is your problem."

Luckily, that was enough for Morgan to drop the subject and they both turned in for bed. Just like the night before, Margie was unable to sleep. She tossed and turned in her bed and grew strained with every passing hour. For a while she'd feel hot, then she'd throw off the covers and grow cold and repeat the process. She didn't know what to do; it felt like this secret was eating her alive.

There *was* someone she could talk to about it, though she wasn't sure if he already knew. Hank would understand. More importantly, she trusted Hank. He would know what to do – or at least, he'd be able to give her an idea of how to proceed. Hank went from being her only friend on the island to something more. A flutter took off in her stomach. Of course she could talk to him.

What *was* it about him? He'd kind of snuck up on her. The thought that he was interested in her didn't even cross her mind until he invited her on that boat! And then they had such a lovely time.

Margie smiled to herself – he wasn't a bad looking man, either. Sure, he was a little soft around the middle – but so was she. And she could close her eyes and see him chopping up that wood. He was so strong. So honest and sincere.

So different than Jeff.

The next morning, she stopped by the Sheriff's Department to see if Hank was in. She was informed that he had taken the entire week off to spend with his daughter. That made sense. And Margie didn't want to just pop over and surprise him. His daughter seemed a bit annoyed when she dropped in on their dinner.

She sat in her car in the parking lot and sent him a message. "Hi Hank, I hope you're having a nice visit with Amanda. I hate to bother you, but I want to talk to you about something. Something important. Can we meet for lunch this week?"

He didn't respond for a few hours, which Margie found surprising. Before when they texted back and forth, he answered right away. She reasoned he must be busy with Amanda.

Then she read his response, several hours later. "Hey Margie, I'm sorry but that won't be possible this week. I'm sure that one of the deputies can help you out if you're having any trouble. Take care."

One of the deputies? Take care? What was that supposed to mean? That made it sound like he was saying goodbye forever.

Margie felt beads of sweat collecting on her forehead. Was this a hot flash? Or did Hank already know about Morgan and Jeff, and he hated her for lying to him?

No, she couldn't let that stand. He deserved to hear the full story before he could hate her for it. When she first saw the picture, she went into a sort of shock. It was even worse than when Morgan appeared at her door. When she regained her senses, she thought about telling Morgan right away and just coming clean. Telling her that she hadn't known for sure until then.

But that left a lot of open questions. Why had Jeff done what he'd done? She needed a chance to talk to him in private. It was too awful to accept that he could have been so cruel and knowingly abandoned Morgan.

If he knew all along, then the man that she chose to be the father of her children was a terrible person. It meant that she put up with his endless traveling and mood swings for nothing. It meant that she was the biggest fool in the world.

What she wanted to know most dearly was if Kelly ever told Jeff that she was pregnant. There was a chance that her visit to the house on that fateful night was her first attempt to tell him, and her last.

What if she hadn't expected to see Margie there? Or, what if she'd just found out that Jeff was married, and heartbroken, she showed up at the house?

Truth be told, it wasn't out of the realm of possibility that Jeff had some sort of a fling when they were young. Margie hated to admit it – to face it, really – but clearly, something like that occurred. It seemed impossible, though, that he would have knowingly abandoned Kelly and Morgan. It just... couldn't be.

She needed a chance to talk to Jeff first, to show him Kelly's picture. If she told Morgan that Jeff was her father before knowing exactly what happened, she ran the risk of hurting Morgan *more* than if she waited to get the full story.

She'd hoped she could wait to do it in person, but now she saw how foolish that was. Margie took a deep breath and pulled out her phone. She dialed Jeff's number.

No answer.

She decided to leave a voicemail – something light, but making it clear that they needed to talk. Hopefully he'd call back soon and they could have this very difficult conversation.

Until then, Margie decided to focus on getting the house and the barn ready for the party. That was all she could do to not go crazy with the secret hanging over her.

Chapter 16

"I don't see why we have to spend the night there," said Brandon, arms firmly crossed on his chest.

He was tired, and the last thing he wanted to do was be forced to make pleasant conversation with his mother-in-law and that annoying girl.

"I thought it might be easier, so we didn't have to rush to catch the ferry. My mom is going to make dinner. Plus, I told Morgan that I'd go on a hike with her and..." Jade's voice trailed off.

Brandon sighed. It didn't seem necessary to *him* for them to have to sleep on San Juan Island. He'd planned to relax and watch a movie that night.

Ever since Jade started going over to her mom's more often, it was actually really nice for him – he had a lot more time to himself. But when he had to do things like this – go all the way to San Juan for *no* reason – he wondered if it was worth it.

Jade spoke again. "I mean, we don't have to stay the night if you don't want to. I just thought that it might be nicer."

"No, we're already going, so it doesn't matter. I don't know why you always run with these ideas and don't tell me about them. It's really not fair."

"I did tell you, I thought you agreed it was a good idea too."

Brandon sat up. His back hurt, and the seats on the ferry were uncomfortable. "Yeah, I was kind of okay with it before I realized that you wanted me to DJ your dad's party for free. Now I'm just losing valuable time that I could be working."

Jade laughed. "Oh come on, you didn't have anything booked for that night."

"But maybe I *could* have."

"Listen, I never said that you were going to do it for free, but I just thought...well, it'd be a nice gift for my dad if you did."

Of course. What was *she* getting him? That would be like her setting up a whole website for free or something. "Jade, I'm an artist. I can't just give away my services for free."

She sighed. "Fine. Then I'll pay your normal rate."

He tilted his head. "What's with the attitude? Why have you been acting like this recently?"

"Like what? I just think that –"

"You're being so manipulative, making me do your dad's party."

"I thought that you said that you wanted to get in on the ground level, so that you could be the DJ for all of the events that my mom will have at the barn."

He shrugged. He may have said *something* like that, but it wasn't what he meant. "I just can't talk about this right now."

Brandon walked upstairs to get himself a soda. Jade was always holding him back. None of the other DJs that he knew would just do some old man's boring birthday. That was ridiculous. And of course her mom would use him for all of her events – why wouldn't she? Who else would come out to the stupid island? Didn't she *want* him to succeed? Or was she as against him as Jade was?

He spent the rest of the ferry ride listening to music on his phone. When it was time to get off, Jade found him and outstretched a hand.

"Brandon honey – I'm really sorry. Can we please just try and have a nice time?"

He sighed. "I guess. But I'm not going hiking with you guys. My back hurts."

"Are you sure? I don't want to leave you behind."

Nothing new there! She was always leaving him behind. He was out there busting his tail to make a name for himself, and she was doing what? Working her easy job at the bank. Hanging out with her mom and eating bonbons. Typical Jade – she'd never understand how hard he worked.

"It's fine."

As soon as they got to Margie's house, Morgan started annoying him. She was way too excited to go on this hike and already had a bag packed with snacks.

"Are you sure you don't want to come? I packed enough snacks for three people. And I packed a bottle of wine, to make it fancy!"

Brandon nodded. "I'm sure, you girls have fun. I'm gonna sit here and relax for a bit."

"Aw," Jade said, delicately trying to hold his hand. "I was hoping I could spend more time with you."

"Well maybe you should've thought of that before deciding to go on this hike without me," he said in a low voice. "It's fine. I'll just hang out in one of the spare rooms until your mom gets home."

"No, really, I'll stay here with you…"

He sighed. Jade was being clingy again. He hated when she was like this – she would follow him around and keep whining until he made her feel better.

"No really, it's fine. I just need to take a break. I'll see you later."

To his relief, she did what he told her to do and left for the hike with Morgan. It was actually better this way – he had a couple of podcasts that he hadn't had time to listen to.

He was able to listen to his first podcast in peace, but about twenty minutes into the second one, the front door opened. He didn't feel like talking to Margie, so he quickly got up and closed the bedroom door. He could pretend like he was sleeping so that he didn't have to spend any unnecessary time talking to his mother-in-law.

He settled himself back on the bed. This new mattress was pretty comfortable – at least maybe he'd get a good night of sleep. He put his headphones back on but it was no use – he could hear Margie droning on in the kitchen. Who was she even talking to?

He got up, ready to tell her to keep it down, when something caught his ear.

"They could come home any minute, and I don't want them to hear what I'm about to tell you."

Brandon quietly sat down on the ground near the door. Now *this* could be something interesting.

Margie continued. "No, no, I definitely have time to talk. I'm just saying – I probably have to make it quick. But I'm so glad that you called Sandy, I've really missed you."

It was quiet for a moment – Margie appeared to be listening to something that her sister Sandy was saying. He leaned in closer to the door to make sure that he didn't miss anything.

"Oh yeah, I'm sure that Mike's fine. You know how he is." Another pause. "I know, I couldn't believe he sold it to me either! It was a total surprise. You have to visit. Okay, right, let me tell you what's going on..."

Brandon made sure he was entirely still so he wouldn't make any noise. Margie took a deep breath before speaking again. "This all started over twenty years ago..."

The story went on for over ten minutes. Brandon rolled his eyes – Margie was so annoying when she had something to say – she never just got to the point. Sometimes Margie and Jade talked back and forth like a pair of birds.

But she was talking so quickly – he'd never even heard her talk so fast before. At first, he wasn't exactly sure what she was talking about. The dead woman showed up at her door a long time ago?

Who cares? But then it got good – so good that Brandon couldn't believe what he was hearing. Apparently, Margie's hospitality to that annoying girl Morgan wasn't just her being nice. Morgan was Jeff's kid! And Margie hadn't told anybody. Not even Morgan knew.

Margie was hemming and hawing over what to do when she said, "Oh shoot, I have to go Sandy. Jade is calling me!"

It gave Brandon a chance to quietly get back on the bed so he could pretend like he was sleeping. He stretched out and mulled over what he'd just heard.

First of all, this was unbelievable. The whole thing was ridiculous. Did Morgan think she could just waltz in here and get an inheritance from Jeff? Jeff was a really wealthy guy – he was bound to leave his money to his kids.

Sure, he had a bunch of girlfriends, but he never made the mistake of marrying one of them again. He learned that lesson in the divorce when he had to pay alimony to Margie.

Hopefully when he died, he would leave his money to his kids. Brandon didn't think that Tiffany even needed the money – she was a hotshot in Chicago. And what was Connor going to do with money? That dude would be happy living in a tent in the woods.

Really, Jade and Brandon needed it the most. They were the ones that needed to buy a house. They were the ones that were going to have to take care of Margie in her old age, obviously, since she moved herself up here.

Brandon laid on the bed, staring up at the ceiling. He could feel his face growing hot. He was so angry about the situation. If this Morgan girl made a big fuss about Jeff being her dad, who knows what would happen? Maybe she would get a bunch of his money.

And why was Margie trying to figure out how to talk to Jeff about it? She said he hadn't called her back, even though she called him three times. Couldn't she take the hint?

Was she going to shame him into accepting this girl as his daughter? Was she really naïve enough to think that Jeff didn't know, that it was some big mistake? Obviously Jeff knew. Obviously he told Kelly that he wouldn't give her a dime all those years ago. That's what Brandon would've done in that situation. Sometimes mistakes happen, but you don't have to ruin your entire life over them.

The front door opened and Brandon could hear Morgan and Jade's voices. Shoot – he had to join them soon. He had to act natural around them; nobody could know what was going on or what he knew. Not until he had a plan of what to do with this information.

It only took a few minutes before Jade came looking for him.

"There you are! Are you feeling okay?"

He sat up, rubbing his eyes. "Oh wow, I must've fallen asleep. Yeah, I feel a lot better."

Margie appeared in the doorway. "Oh my goodness! I didn't even know that you were here Brandon."

He rubbed his eyes again with the palms of his hands. He needed to make a show of it. "Yeah, so sorry about that. I didn't even hear any of you guys come home. I was out like a light. Just been working so much recently."

"He has been," said Jade, rubbing his shoulder.

He put a hand on top of hers. "But I feel better now, thanks honey."

"Well, I'm gonna go and make dinner. You kids just relax until then. I hope I didn't wake you up," said Margie.

She looked nervous. Good. She should be.

"No, not at all, I was so tired I just passed out."

Margie nodded. "Oh, okay. Well – dinner will be ready soon."

Brandon turned to his wife. "How was the hike? I hope Morgan didn't drive you too crazy."

Jade shushed him. "Not at all. You should really give her a chance, she's very nice."

Darn. It seemed like making Jade one of his allies was going to be tough. She had a soft spot for the girl. Jade was like her mom – she was too nice. People manipulated her.

"Well," he said in a low voice, "she gives me a bad feeling. I can't put my finger on it."

Jade frowned. "Just give her a chance, please? For me?"

He smiled. "Anything for you sweetheart."

Chapter 17

The rest of Amanda's visit went well. There was no more mention of Margie, and therefore, no further exchange of heated words. As planned, on Corinne's birthday, Hank and Amanda took the boat out and visited all of their favorite places. They arranged a time and made a video call to Jacob, so he could join them in commemorating the day.

It was hard saying goodbye to Amanda when it was time for her to go back to London; she promised to visit again soon, and again reiterated her invitation for Hank to come to London.

"You don't want your old man putting a damper on your style," he said.

She rolled her eyes. "Dad, I have *way* too much style for that to be a problem."

Hank laughed. He wasn't really sure where Amanda got her smart mouth – it certainly wasn't from him, and Corinne was as sweet natured as a person could be. Hank suspected that it came from his own mother, a firecracker who passed away before Amanda was even born.

Though Amanda's lively spirit was difficult at times when she was a teenager, he still loved her for it. It reminded him so much of his mom, and he liked that she had some fight in her. She never let the world get her down.

Hank however was always a softy, and it seemed he'd been getting softer as the years went on. He could feel the tears coming to his eyes as he watched her get ready to drive to the ferry. "Are you sure you don't want me to come with you? Maybe the ferry will be late and we can grab a coffee or something."

Amanda shook her head. "No, it's okay, I don't want you to go through the trouble. How about if it's late I give you a call?"

He nodded. "Alright sweetie. Well, have a safe trip."

She wrapped her arms around his neck. "Don't cry Dad, I'll see you again soon, okay?"

"Okay, take care."

He watched her drive away. A call to join her in Friday Harbor never came. After waiting a half hour, he took a deep breath and decided to put himself to use.

He was able to busy himself for a few hours with cleaning up the house, but then he was left to his own thoughts and the ever present silence. He pulled out his phone to see if maybe Margie had written him back – she hadn't.

Hank felt bad that he had sent her such a cold message, but what was he supposed to do? Amanda was right. It was wrong for him to start a relationship with someone new. Maybe he and Margie could be friends someday, but while he still had such strong feelings for her, he needed to stay away.

He went back to work the next day and tried to invest his attention on whatever was handed to him. There was a complaint about illegal fireworks – he investigated that without resolution. Someone on the east side of the island put in a call about some deer that looked sick. Hank wasn't able to find any. He ticketed a record sixteen people for not wearing their seat belts. All in all – nothing exciting.

There was one piece of good news – apparently Frankie, Brock's mechanic, got into some legal trouble after being caught selling parts from a stolen car. Hank decided it was time to make another visit to him and see if some pressure would loosen his lips.

Unfortunately, when he went to Frankie's shop in Anacortes, it was locked up and dark. No one was inside. He'd have to find where Frankie was hiding; maybe the promise of some leniency would encourage him to be more cooperative about the Kelly Allen case.

The coming Saturday was the day that Hank dreaded most – he even considered picking up a shift just to have something to keep his mind busy, but decided against it. It was the anniversary of Corinne's death. Before she passed away, she made them promise that they would only celebrate her birthday and not the day of her death; she died only ten days after her birthday.

"I told you that I would see forty-five," she'd said.

He sat in the kitchen that morning, remembering how small she looked the day that she passed away. Eating was difficult by then, but Hank bought a birthday cake anyway. She made her best effort to take a few bites. And after that day, she faded so quickly – it really was like she'd held on just to make it to her birthday. And even though Hank knew that she was sick, and that logically, her time was coming, he wasn't ready to let her go.

Hank stared into the black coffee in front of him. It was too bad that Amanda couldn't stay just a bit longer so they could be together for this day. He had no appetite and didn't want to mope around, so he decided to take the boat out and revisit all of Corinne's favorite spots – the places where he'd spread her ashes.

He got started early because he couldn't sleep – just after 7 AM. He decided to head north and loop around Stuart Island, then head south to get to Lime Kiln. Before he got there, though, he cut the boat's engine just short of Posey Island.

It was a tiny little thing – only an acre – and it was a beautiful day. He was surprised to see that there was no one on the island; the island itself was a state park and almost always had visitors.

When the kids were little, they used to rent one of the campsites on Posey and do overnight trips with tent camping. It wasn't that far from home, but the kids thought it was a great adventure. Corinne always packed everything so perfectly – she brought hot dogs and cheeseburgers to make over the fire; she brought all the S'mores supplies for the kids. She'd even sneak in a few beers for them to share once the kids went to bed; they'd just sit quietly, enjoying the crackles from the fire.

Hank wished that he had brought a kayak out with him so he could actually get on the island; there was no dock for the boat. He took a deep breath. He could feel the tears pricking at his eyes. He was never a crier – not until Corinne passed away. Now he felt weak, or softened maybe – like old worn leather.

At least no one was there – Hank was entirely by himself.

"I really miss you, you know," he said out loud. "The kids miss you too. But they're doing okay. They're doing really well, actually. Better than me – which is good. I want them to be happy. Amanda has the great career that she's always dreamed of in London. And Jacob – well, Jacob applied to every tech company in Australia just to see who would take him. He loves it there. You would've loved it, too. The beaches are right up your alley. I think he might even have a girlfriend that he's not telling me about." Hank laughed, shaking his head.

He sat for a moment, feeling the soft rock of the boat in the waves.

"To tell you the truth, I still haven't really figured out how to live without you. I go to work, I do things around the house. I finally painted that door you hated." He laughed again. "Everything else looks the same, the weather is the same, the tourists follow the same patterns...but somehow, everything is so different without you. It's like I'm living on a different planet now where everything looks right, but nothing feels right. I just don't..."

His voice broke. "I don't know what to do. You always knew the answer, you always did the right thing. You were the one with the plan, not me. I feel like a toy with the batteries left on, just doing the things I'm supposed to do, but there's no reason for it."

Hank looked around to make sure that he was still alone. He was – there wasn't a single kayaker, or boat of whale watchers, or even a single seagull. There was not another living soul who could hear him.

He cleared his throat. "I know that you told me you wanted me to find a way to be happy again. For me to find someone else. Unbelievably, I met someone, and – well, I don't know how she feels about me, but once Amanda even caught a *whiff* of it, she was – well, she was herself. But she's right. You've only been gone for two years. It feels like a lifetime, but it's only been two years. And we were together for *twenty-seven years*. I don't even know a life without you. And it was wrong of me to even think of a life without you."

Hank paused – he thought he heard something. No, it couldn't be. Or...was it?

Then he heard it again: the breath of a killer whale. He looked up and saw a pod, their breaths misting in the sunshine. They were only a few hundred feet from his boat, and they were coming right for him. He double checked that his engine was off.

Within moments, an entire pod of orcas surrounded his boat. At first he thought they were just passing by, but they lingered – spy hopping, jumping, slapping their tails against the water. They were playing, they were celebrating. It was unbelievably loud, and Hank could hardly hear himself laughing over their ruckus. And he was in the middle of it all.

He'd seen this at a distance before, of course, but never so close. He ran to the side of the boat and peered over just as an orca swam beneath him. He could make out the white eye patch and even the orca's small eye – he felt something stir in his soul. He'd never seen an orca that close up before – the little eye looked so wise. He had to remind himself to breathe. They were throwing a loud and boisterous party, and he was smack dab in the middle of it.

Everywhere he turned, the orcas were loudly playing. There was even a small baby who kept bobbing her head to take a peek at him. If Corinne were there, she'd be able to identify them based on their markings. But Hank had no idea who he was seeing – were they residents? Were they transients? Which pod were they from?

It didn't matter, but Corinne would've known them down to the pod. She would've known who the matriarch was, how old she was, how old the baby was. All he could do was stand there, mouth hanging open, in awe. With each splash and water break, it felt like something on his chest was lifting. The heaviness that he brought with him onto the water dissipated. It was replaced with something he hadn't felt in ages.

Something that felt like joy.

Then, just as quickly as they appeared, they disappeared under the black waters. He watched as a handful resurfaced a few hundred feet away, continuing on with their day.

Hank had to sit down. He couldn't believe what just happened – in all of his years living on San Juan, he never experienced anything quite like that. He sat for a moment, absorbing the silence. It was so quiet, he could almost convince himself that they hadn't actually appeared – but they *did!* They were alive, they were real, and they were amazing.

"You have *got* to be kidding me!" Hank yelled. He started to laugh, quietly at first, then it was out of his control. He laughed until his stomach hurt and tears streamed down his face.

Hank was never the sort of man to look for signs – he was logical, pragmatic. Corinne always teased him about it, and he'd tell her that it was how he had to think as a deputy. But there was something undeniably magical about that moment. He was *literally* pleading with his wife, and it seemed that she sent her favorite animal on earth to rescue him.

Hank started the boat. No, this wasn't something he could tell anyone about. Not even his kids. They would think that he really went crazy. But in his heart, he knew what it meant. There was no doubt in his mind that Corinne sent those whales. Her voice rang in his head, "That's enough grumping around. Time to perk up! There's a new day to be had."

He pointed the boat towards home. He had an apology to make.

Chapter 18

Though she felt uneasy that Brandon was in the house when she told her sister about Morgan, Margie didn't have much time to dwell on it. Jeff's surprise party was only a week away, and she had a lot to get done before then. And besides, it seemed like Brandon was sound asleep. What was the chance he even heard anything?

After they left the next morning, Margie decided to finish setting up the furniture in all of the bedrooms before the weekend of the party. Her plan was to give Connor his own room, and Jade and Tiffany would share a room; Jade actually insisted on it. It made Margie happy that the girls got along so well now, because when they were younger, they were always fighting. They finally started to behave like sisters the past few years.

Jade said that while everyone else was in the house, Brandon preferred to have a blow up mattress to himself in the finished basement downstairs; she thought it would be better for him to have somewhere private for a retreat.

"You know how he is," Jade said with a laugh. "He needs his alone time."

As she set up the air mattress, Margie couldn't help but run that comment through her mind over and over. Brandon needed a *lot* of things – not the least of which was to stop being a brat and start behaving like an adult.

Margie thought that at some point with his poor spending habits and bad attitude, Jade might actually put her foot down. Unfortunately, it wasn't in Jade's nature to put her foot down. It was much more in her nature to treat him with never ending kindness.

Margie finished setting up Brandon's bed and tried to shake him out of her mind. It was difficult, especially because the last time that they visited, Brandon was especially critical of Jade. Margie wasn't a violent woman, but the way he spoke to Jade sometimes gave her the urge to jump up and smack him.

As always, though, she resisted that urge. More for Jade's benefit than for Brandon's. If only she'd known what a crummy guy he was all those years ago, maybe she could have convinced Jade to break things off...

Margie set it out of her mind and spent the rest of the week preparing for the party. She put finishing touches on the barn, made the house sparkle and finalized all of the details with the caterer. To Margie's relief, Tammy offered to pay for all of the food at the party. It wasn't that Margie was broke or anything – not *quite* yet – but she certainly needed to start booking some events, or she'd be in trouble.

Her plan was to get the word out about the barn once the party was done. The website for Saltwater Cove was up and running, complete with a brochure, and Morgan's pictures looked amazing.

Jade also set up a website for Jeff's party guests. It told them a bit about the island, what to do for fun, and where Jeff and Tammy would be staying, so that they could avoid running into them before the surprise.

Tammy was adamant that Jeff couldn't see anyone before the actual surprise party. Even Margie wasn't allowed to speak to Jeff beforehand – much to her dismay.

"No!" Tammy said immediately. "You'll have to be there to surprise him with everyone else!"

It was impossible; Margie definitely wasn't going to tell Tammy what was going on with Morgan. And it seemed that Tammy wasn't going to budge. Margie settled on speaking to Jeff as soon as possible.

It could have been worse. Initially, Morgan volunteered to be the party photographer as a sort of present. Margie avoided discussing that with her for a long time – she couldn't think of how to tell her no. Then, out of nowhere, a stroke of luck hit: Morgan's dad decided that he was coming up that very same weekend to visit.

"I feel so bad that I won't be there like I said I would be," said Morgan.

Margie was adamant. "No, absolutely *do not* feel bad. We'll have plenty of pictures, and you need to have fun with your dad!"

"He's just coming out for the weekend, so I think I'll stay with him so I can be out of your hair. He told me I've overstayed my welcome with you."

"Don't say that!" replied Margie. "You're always a welcome part of the family."

Morgan smiled, but didn't seem to feel the weight Margie put on those words.

On Friday, Tiffany and Connor arrived on the same ferry. Margie anxiously waited at the ferry landing.

"Hey guys! Over here!"

Connor caught sight of her and excitedly waved. Tiffany dipped her sunglasses down and waved. She looked fabulous – high heels, a pinstriped dress and a black blazer. Margie giggled to herself – she thought Tiffany looked great, but she also knew that if Jade were there, she would've teased her for looking so "city" as she called it.

"Hey Mom!" Connor pulled her in for a hug.

"Hi sweetheart." She squeezed him tightly, then hugged Tiffany.

"We haven't been here in *forever*," Tiffany commented. "How is it possible that it looks *exactly* the same?"

Margie laughed. "Wait until you see Uncle Mike's old house. And the barn! It's all different."

"Did you do it all yourself?" asked Connor as he loaded their luggage into the back of the car.

"No," Margie said slowly. "I had some professionals do the tough stuff – the plumbing, the electric. I had one contractor who gave me a hard time, but a friend of mine went and – well, eventually he finished the job."

"And that girl? The one that's living with you?" asked Tiffany.

"Yes, Morgan. Morgan Allen. She's been staying with me, and she's been a big help too."

Connor cocked his head to the side. "Did I hear about this?"

"I'm sure I told you honey, she's the girl whose mom was killed on the island by a drunk driver a few months ago."

"Oh yeah," he said. "Did they ever find who did it?"

"Sadly, no. Well, they think it was this drunk driver. But I know the police are still working on it."

Just then, Margie remembered that Hank had sent her two text messages. She completely forgot to answer – it wasn't intentional at all, but it might seem that way to him. She was in the middle of something when the messages came through. Margie bit her lip and reminded herself to answer him when she got home.

Yet as soon as they got home, Margie forgot about responding again, and instead got swept up in showing Tiffany and Connor the property. They were both impressed by the barn's transformation, and Tiffany appreciated the feminine touches that Margie brought into the home. Connor was most astonished by the beautiful view of the ocean.

"I think Uncle Mike must've cleared some trees out of here," he commented. "Whenever we used to visit, I don't think that you could see out like this."

Margie nodded. "That's entirely possible."

As they got settled in the house, an unexpected guest arrived: Morgan.

Margie's heart rate picked up when she saw her come through the door. How would her kids react to their half-sister?

"Hi everyone!" said Morgan. "I've heard so much about both of you, I feel like I know you already."

Oh boy. Hopefully Jade had a chance to tell Tiffany how much she liked Morgan; Tiffany did not take making friends lightly.

Tiffany smiled and offered a handshake. "It's nice to meet you too. Morgan, right?"

"Yes, that's me!"

Connor came over and started talking with a mouth full of cookies. "Nice to meet you, I'm Connor."

Margie looked at the three of them standing there and felt momentarily frozen. She shook herself out of it. "Morgan, isn't your dad supposed to arrive soon?"

"Oh yeah, I didn't get to tell you. His flight was canceled. Now he's not coming until tomorrow in the afternoon. But he was able to get off of work on Monday, so he just extended his stay a bit."

"Where is he traveling from?" asked Tiffany.

Margie took the chance to step away. This wasn't good – not at all. What if Morgan wanted to hang around the barn and take pictures now as the party started? She absolutely *could not* see Jeff before Margie had a chance to talk to him – and then to Morgan, too! It was a very delicate matter, and Margie didn't want anything to go wrong.

She looked up – the kids were still talking, and Connor was saying something about how much he loved the Oregon coast. Margie pulled her phone out – it was time to finally answer Hank.

"I'm very sorry I didn't write back sooner – things have been so hectic and it completely slipped my mind. Would you have just a few minutes to chat? I have a big favor to ask you."

His reply came almost instantly. "Of course. Do you want me to call you? Or I can stop by if that's better."

She didn't want there to be any chance of the kids overhearing her. She popped her head into their conversation. "Hey, I just need to run to the store to grab a few things. I'll be right back, okay?

"Okay!" They answered before getting back to talking.

Margie rushed to her car, and once the door was securely closed, she called Hank.

He picked up after two rings. "Hello?"

"Hi Hank. The thing I need to talk to you about is...a little strange. I was thinking that maybe we could meet. I could even stop by your place if that's convenient?"

"Oh! Sure, that would be fine. When were you thinking?"

"I was thinking...right now?"

Hank laughed. "Luckily my place is still pretty clean from Amanda's visit. Come on over, I'll send you the address."

Margie got off the phone and anxiously waited for his text. It was true that she needed to stop by the grocery store – but it could've waited until tomorrow. She felt bad lying about it – but she felt bad about *everything* right now. They just needed to get through the next twenty-four hours without any major catastrophes and then everything would be out in the open.

Hank's address came through and Margie plugged it into her GPS. It was only a few minutes away, which was a relief. Despite the short drive, it felt like it took forever to get there.

Margie hopped out of her car immediately after parking. Hank was ready for her – he appeared at the front door almost instantly.

"Hey! It's nice to see you."

She smiled. "Thanks for having me on such short notice. I promise this won't take long."

"No, please." He opened the door for her. "I have nothing else to do, and I'd love to give you the tour, and actually, there was something that I needed to..."

"I'm sorry Hank, I don't have a lot of time. I don't want the kids to get suspicious. But I have a strange favor to ask you."

"Anything you need."

Oh wow. That seemed very...resolute. What if she was going to ask him to do something awful? What if she wanted a million dollars, or to ask him to egg Jeff's car?

"Well, I can't really tell you the full story yet. But I will, I promise. I don't mean to be so secretive, it's just that it's not my secret to tell, and first..." Her voice trailed off.

He put his hands up. "There's no need to explain. I trust you."

Well. Margie felt a little flutter in her chest. That didn't sound like the words of a man who despised her. Maybe he hadn't found out about Morgan's paternity? Maybe he was just busy or something. For him to say something like that definitely made it seem like he didn't hate her. But when she finally told him the truth, there was no way he'd trust her again.

"I need you to keep Morgan away from the surprise party tomorrow. Again, I promise that I'll explain why later, it's just that –"

"No problem. I can talk to her about her mom's case or something."

Margie cringed. "Uh, maybe not something so sensitive?"

"You're right," Hank said with a frown. "Not my best idea. I can take her on a ride along?"

"Oh! You're on duty tomorrow?"

"Yeah, so I can pitch that to her. Do you need her to be busy the entire night too?"

Margie shook her head. "No, her dad should be coming at some point tomorrow, so just until then. But she just *can't* come to the party. Or see the guests."

Hank studied her for a moment, but if he had any doubts, he wasn't showing them. "Okay. I can stop by tomorrow morning and see if I can get her to bite."

"Actually," Margie twisted her hands together. "I was hoping that you could stop over right now. And just act like – well, you know, that it just came to you? Or something?"

"Oh." Hank shrugged. "Sure, no problem. Anything you need. I can head over now."

Margie bit her lip. "But won't that look suspicious? That we both get back there at the same time?"

Hank cracked a smile. "You evil masterminds think of everything, don't you?"

"No," said Margie with a sigh. "Unfortunately not. Okay, I'm actually going to run to the store so I have something to bring back. I told them that I was going to the store."

"An airtight alibi," quipped Hank.

She suppressed a smile. This wasn't funny. But seeing him again was nice.

"And you can come, in maybe like, an hour or so? Oh! Stop by for dinner. My son and daughter just got in, and I'm making a pot roast."

"Say no more, you're right, one of your amazing dinners is the perfect excuse as to why I would randomly stop over."

Margie laughed. "Thanks Hank. You're a lifesaver. I'll see you soon."

She got back in her car and headed to the store. As nervous as she was about this entire situation, she felt calmed by the fact that now she had Hank on her side. He seemed so unwaveringly loyal too. It was...nice. He put on a tough guy image, but he was quite a lovely man.

Glad that she had an ally, Margie set out to finish the rest of her plan.

Chapter 19

It was a bit awkward talking to Tiffany, but Morgan found Connor to be an open book. She kind of expected them to be that way – Jade told her all about how they were growing up and how they were now.

"Tiffany's really serious. So sometimes she can come off as...I don't know, harsh?" Jade told her. "But she's not harsh, not at all. She has a really good heart. She's just...careful. She doesn't open up to people easily."

Morgan wasn't so sure about Jade's judgments – it seemed that sometimes, Jade gave people the benefit of the doubt who didn't deserve it. Brandon, for example, wasn't the friendliest guy, but Jade seemed to adore him. Maybe that was the plight of overly nice people: they attracted outcasts, people who nobody else could put up with. They could see the good in them, but no one else could.

That was how Morgan's mom always was. She tried to teach Morgan to look for the best in people – even though this theory often led to her being taken advantage of. She was trusting, and even if someone did use her, or lie to her, she didn't get angry. Not really.

Morgan got angry on her behalf. In fact, Morgan felt angry most of the time now. She couldn't believe that the police still hadn't proven that Brock killed her mom. She knew that Chief

Hank was trying, but he was pretty tight lipped about updates. He probably thought they were never going to solve it and she should just let it go.

But how could she? The last week, Morgan went into Friday Harbor and made a plea to every business owner in the area asking if they had camera footage from the night her mom died. They told her that they would look into it, but so far no one called or emailed.

There was one possible breakthrough – Morgan spent an entire day going up and down the surrounding streets and talking to homeowners, too. It turned out many of them kept cameras on their properties. Some were simple doorbell cameras, but others were complete security systems. Everyone she spoke to said they were willing to look back and see if they still had recordings from that night. With all those cameras, someone *had* to have something.

"What did you go to school for?"

Morgan startled. She didn't realize that Tiffany was talking to her because she was lost in her own thoughts. "History. But I still have a semester to finish. I left school after my mom died."

Connor's face fell. "Oh. I'm so sorry to hear that."

"It's okay, I can go back." Morgan didn't want to depress the mood, even though she was very good at doing that. "It's just...hard. And what am I going to do with a history degree anyway?"

Tiffany and Connor both laughed. Good – she had to remind herself not to weave her mom's death into every conversation. But it was tough, because to her, it felt like everything in her life was still entangled with the tragedy. It was almost all she could think about, even though the rest of the world moved on.

Margie got back not too long after that and Morgan insisted on helping with dinner; she wanted Margie to be able to spend some time with her kids. Just as dinner was being served, Chief Hank showed up. It was almost as though he had a sixth sense for good food.

"I hope I'm not being a bother!" he said as he sat down.

Morgan had to force herself not to smile. She thought he *definitely* meant to be a bother. His adoration for Margie was obvious to everyone but Margie – though it seemed like she might finally be starting to catch on.

It was sweet – Margie was a really nice person. Hank seemed like he was too. He didn't arrest her, after all. She owed him one.

Dinner was delicious, and before Morgan had a chance to jump up and start collecting plates, Chief Hank said he had a proposition for her.

"Are you busy tomorrow? I wanted to take you for a ride along."

Morgan bit her lip. "That's really nice of you, but my dad is coming in, and I was going to take some pictures of the party for Margie."

"Oh please, don't miss out on fun on my behalf," said Margie. "You can even pick up your dad in the police car. Wouldn't that be fun?"

Morgan laughed. "Yeah, I guess. Except I don't want the poor man to have a heart attack."

She carried a stack of dishes into the kitchen. Maybe it wouldn't be the worst thing in the world to hang out with Chief Hank. He might be able to pressure the people with cameras to actually look into their records. Maybe he even knew them personally – he seemed to know everyone on this island.

There was a chance that he might get angry with her for trying to find things on her own...so maybe it was best not to involve him. But if she *did* find a recording showing Brock driving along the road, maybe even striking her mom, would Brock then accuse her of tampering with the evidence?

As if she knew how to tamper with a video! A picture, sure, but not a video.

Still, it wasn't worth the risk in case it did actually become evidence. She decided she'd come clean to Chief Hank.

When she got back to the dining room she said, "Okay Chief, that sounds like fun. I'm in."

A smile spread across his face. "Alright! It *will* be fun. You'll see."

That night, Morgan was supposed to sleep at the place that her dad rented, but since he didn't make it to the island, it seemed a bit weird to go and sleep there by herself. Luckily, Margie insisted that she stay the night with them. It was nice because she didn't have to rush out after dinner. Chief Hank stayed behind too, because Connor asked him to tell some stories about all the crazy things he'd seen as a deputy.

They sat on the couches in the living room as the Chief told them about some of the stupid (and hilarious) things people did to get themselves involved with the deputies. Everyone thought it was great – except maybe Tiffany, who sat quietly on the end of the couch. She laughed sometimes, politely, but not real laughs.

She was so different than Jade, and Morgan felt insecure around her. Since Tiffany didn't say much, Morgan couldn't work out what she was thinking – so naturally, she defaulted to thinking that Tiffany must not like her.

Morgan wasn't quiet and she wasn't used to quiet people – she'd often say things that came into her head without filtering it first. And it wasn't that everyone had to be just like her, but if Tiffany were just a *bit* more open, it would've been nice.

When Chief Hank left, Morgan excused herself to go to bed. She felt a bit like an intruder, and she wanted Margie to get to spend time with her family. Morgan went to her room and shut the door, checking her email and her phone for any messages about videos.

Still nothing. She drifted off to sleep.

The next morning, Jade and Brandon arrived early, their car stuffed with DJ equipment. Morgan was excited to see Jade, and headed into the kitchen first thing. Rather quickly, though, she looked for a way to excuse herself; she found herself in the middle of a loud, boisterous reunion between Jade, Tiffany, and Connor, and it made her feel rather awkward.

She waved hello before grabbing a banana and heading back to her room. She needed to get ready for her ride along anyhow – Chief said that he wanted to pick her up around 9:30. She got dressed, then wasted some time looking at cat pictures on the internet. A bit after nine, she heard a knock on the door.

"Hey, do you have a second?"

Brandon. Ugh.

"Oh, yeah. Just getting ready for my ride along with Chief Hank."

Brandon nodded. "Cool. I was wondering if you could help me set up some of my equipment. Jade would normally help but she's completely ignoring me."

"Uh, sure, I still have some time before he's supposed to get here."

"Great! Thanks. I *really* appreciate it."

Well. Wasn't he being weirdly polite. Only because he needed something, she decided. Jade told her earlier that week that Brandon was having a hard time booking events – there was a lot of competition, apparently. It was probably going to be a big deal for him to be able to do events at Saltwater Cove, and he needed to get it right.

They made their way out to the barn. Morgan paused to admire how beautiful it looked – all of the tables and chairs were set up, along with some decorations. Margie just needed to add the plates and the centerpieces and it would be picture perfect.

Brandon pulled the door of the barn shut and walked over to her. A chill ran down her spine.

"I'm actually really glad that I have a chance to talk to you," he said.

Oh *great*. He was still using his "nice" voice, and he was standing way too close.

She took a step back. "Oh really? What about?"

"Well," Brandon said with a heavy sigh, "I just can't stand what they're doing to you anymore."

"What who is doing to me?"

He pointed in the direction behind her, towards the house. "All of them. Margie, Tiffany, Connor…even Jade. Though she's my wife, and I promise to keep her secrets, I just can't keep this one."

Morgan crossed her arms. "I don't know what you're talking about."

He took a step closer. "I know you don't. It's just that… well, let me show you something."

He pulled out his cell phone and opened up a picture. "Now what I'm about to show you is very shocking. But I think you deserve to know."

Morgan took the phone from his hand and ran her eyes over the picture. It looked like Jade, Tiffany, and Connor when they were younger. A family picture. Margie was there too, looking younger but still very much herself. Behind them all was a dark haired man.

Morgan gasped. "Who is that guy?"

"They didn't tell you." Brandon shook his head. "I knew they were hiding it from you."

Morgan zoomed in on the man's face. "But that's impossible. My mom told me that he died before I was born."

Brandon frowned. "That was a lie. Your mom had no choice – it wasn't her fault. She didn't know that Jeff was married when she...well, fell in love with him. And stuff."

Nausea bucked and rolled in Morgan's stomach. The room felt too hot. "So that's Jeff? Margie's ex-husband?"

Brandon nodded. "Yes. And he's very much alive. He cheated on Margie all those years ago, but Margie took him back. They made a plan that if your mom's baby – you – ever showed up, that they had to...take certain precautions."

Morgan's head was spinning. "I don't understand. Are you saying that..."

"I know, it's a lot to take in. But you're doing *so* well."

Morgan couldn't stop looking at the picture. How was it possible that this man was alive her entire life? And her mom never told her? How could *everyone* lie to her about it?

"I know that you think Margie is this really nice lady, but she's really cut throat. She wanted to make sure that you wouldn't show up and disrupt the image of their perfect family."

Morgan realized that Brandon had his hand on her shoulder.

"Why did they...I mean, why..." She couldn't put her thoughts together.

"I'm really sorry that I had to be the one to tell you this. But they were trying to keep you away from the party so you wouldn't see Jeff before they could put their plan into action. And I mean – I'm just *not* the kind of person who's okay with something like that. I don't care about how it looks. It's so wrong for them to treat you this way."

Morgan shook her head. "I don't even want anything from him. I would just want…"

"I know, I know." Brandon wrapped his arms around her and stroked her back. "But they just don't know how nice of a person you are. They don't deserve you."

Morgan's arms were pinned to her side. She was still clutching the phone in one hand. Brandon smelled weird – like sweat and fruity chewing gum.

She pulled away.

"I'm really sorry that you had to find out this way, but I thought you deserved to know."

She handed him his phone back just as she heard a car pull up. It made two quick honks.

"I think Chief Hank is here to pick me up," she said numbly.

"Well listen – don't say anything to them. Probably the best thing you can do is leave and never speak to any of them again. Make them worry that you found out the plan. Ghost them."

"Ghost them?"

"Yeah, just disappear. Or…you could get revenge on them all."

Two more honks.

"Revenge? I don't...I don't want anything from him." Morgan felt like she was repeating herself. She didn't know what else to say.

Brandon's eyes grew wide for a moment. "I mean – what I meant to say is that the best revenge is living a great life, right?"

She shrugged. "Yeah, I guess."

He pulled the barn door open. "Well, have a good day, okay?"

Morgan nodded and slowly walked out of the barn.

"Hang in there," he called out after her.

She threw a hand up to wave. She didn't want to look back. She didn't want to go hang out with Chief Hank, either, but the alternative was going back inside Margie's house. And that seemed like a bad idea, since as the shock wore off, the anger she was so familiar began to engulf her.

Chapter 20

The morning before the party flew by. Margie had a hundred little details to pull together and not quite enough time to do them all. Jade volunteered to help, which was lovely, and even Tiffany and Connor pitched in. By 4 o'clock, there were still a couple of things they didn't get to, but Margie made everyone stop what they were doing to get ready for the party. The guests were to arrive at 5 o'clock, and Jeff and Tammy would be there at 5:30 sharp.

The cover story was that Tammy really wanted to see where Margie was living now. Apparently, Jeff put up quite the fight with her, saying he didn't want to come along, but Tammy was eventually able to convince him. Margie wasn't sure why Tammy decided to share *that* piece of information with her – she tried not to let it hurt her feelings. Was she really so bad that Jeff wouldn't at least stop by and say hello?

As she got ready, Margie sent a text message to Hank to see how everything was going. Unfortunately, he didn't answer.

Maybe he was busy; she didn't have time to dwell on it. Margie slipped into the light blue dress that she bought for the occasion; she had met Jade on the mainland to go shopping. It was quite a fun day, and Margie loved the dress that she found. She applied a touch of makeup and added a few curls to her hair – nothing too fancy, just a little bit more than usual. She was the hostess, after all and this was the barn's debut event!

Tammy insisted that the guests should not drive themselves so there wouldn't be a bunch of cars parked on the property to signal Jeff that something was going on. Margie certainly had the space for it, but she understood. Instead, a trolley picked up guests at several spots in town and dropped them off at Saltwater Cove. The last drop off was at 5:20. Margie anxiously peaked into the barn – it was full of life, booming with laughter and twinkling lights and excited voices setting the tone.

Margie's heart swelled. It took all summer, but the barn was complete. It was beautiful. She wished that she could send a picture to Mike, but she knew that it was impossible to contact him. She snapped a picture anyway – maybe he would check the website and end up seeing it after all.

She rushed back to the house and waited at the window. Jeff and Tammy didn't arrive on time, which was fine, because there were a few guests who came rather late and ignored the no cars rule. Connor was able to show them where to park so that their cars weren't visible.

Finally, at 5:48, the doorbell rang. Margie checked her reflection in the hallway mirror one last time – nothing was out of place. She took a deep breath and smiled, trying to calm her nerves.

"Hi!" she said as she opened the door.

"Hi, so good to see you!" replied Tammy, immediately going in for a hug.

Jeff offered a nod and a wave. "Hi, good to see you."

"Hello Jeff, so glad you could make it!" Margie ignored his formality and pulled him in for a hug. It wasn't like Tammy had anything to worry about – she was *quite* beyond trying to win him back.

"Of course. Why are you so dressed up? Are you going out clubbing later?" He laughed to himself.

Margie and Tammy exchanged looks, but said nothing.

"I'm, uh, going to dinner with some friends in a bit. But come on in, I'll give you the tour of the house, and then we can take a peek at the barn!"

Margie allowed them to walk in front of her so she could quietly grab her phone off of the table and hit dial. She called Brandon, then hung up. It was his signal to get everyone to quiet down.

Margie made the tour of the house fast and led them outside. For some reason, she felt her heart racing as they approached the barn. It was silly, but she couldn't help it. She didn't know how Jeff was going to react. It didn't seem like he was in a particularly good mood.

They got to the barn and Margie was pleased that they couldn't hear anything – not even a whisper from inside.

"Well come on Jeff, help her with the door!" said Tammy.

Jeff shrugged. "Margie's a big girl, she can handle it."

Margie ignored the comment. Jeff always used to have something to say about what she ate, or how a dress was tight here or tight there. One relief of the divorce was that she didn't have to field those comments about how she looked anymore.

In one swift motion, Margie pulled the door open, revealing the party group as they shouted, "Surprise!"

Jeff's jaw dropped and he looked to Tammy, then back at the crowd. Music started to play, and Margie watched as Jeff disappeared to say hello to everyone.

Well, at least *that* part all worked out. She looked at her phone to see the time. It was just after six; Morgan's dad should have arrived and hopefully, they would be busy for the rest of the night. Margie still felt nervous for some reason. She desperately wanted to get Jeff alone so she could talk to him, but obviously, he'd be in high demand for quite some time. Dinner was being served at seven, and Margie hoped that maybe she could get him alone after that.

She tried her best to relax and not worry about all of the small details that she didn't get to. The barn looked lovely, and people seemed to be enjoying themselves. Margie knew about half of them, but the other half were strangers.

Tammy said that she thought it was smart to invite as many of Jeff's business associates as possible – otherwise he would get upset. Margie felt a bit bad for Tammy – she was rather young, much younger than Jeff, and Margie knew for a fact that Jeff held it over her head.

Margie's friends were astonished that she held no ill will toward Tammy. But how could she? She was a sweet woman who tried her best to keep Jeff happy. No one knew better than Margie how difficult that was.

Tammy insisted on a sit down dinner, which the caterers promised wouldn't be a problem. Dinner was served mostly without a hitch, save for one incident where it seemed that there were not enough vegetarian dishes. Margie was able to field the issues in the catering kitchen she'd had installed in the back of the barn. It was large and gave them plenty of room to figure things out – Margie was pleased with herself for having the idea to have the kitchen – and they found the missing meal.

Before dessert, Margie saw her chance to talk to Jeff alone. She watched as he got up from the table and headed towards the bathroom, and though she felt a bit silly, she stood there and waited for him to come out.

"Oh my gosh!" he said when he opened the door. "You scared me."

"Sorry Jeff, I just really need to talk to you. It's important."

He sighed, watching as a waitress walked by carrying several plates of cake. "Alright, I'm supposed to be on a diet anyway so I should avoid dessert."

Margie led him out of the back of the barn and towards the outlook on the water.

"I don't want anyone to overhear us."

"Oh?" he replied, hands in his pockets. "This sounds serious. Sorry I didn't return your call – it's been really busy recently."

"It's okay." She pulled out her phone and opened a picture of Morgan. Her hands were shaking. "So, I don't really know how to tell you this, but a young woman has been staying with me."

He leaned over and looked at the picture. "Cute kid."

"Her name is Morgan Allen. Her mother was Kelly Allen, who passed away quite tragically on the island a few months ago."

Margie fumbled with her phone, trying to pull up a picture of Kelly Allen. Her hands were so cold, despite the pleasantly warm evening.

Finally, she found it and handed it to him. "The first time that I came to San Juan, when Mike gave me the house, I saw Kelly's picture in the newspaper."

Jeff took the phone from her so he could look more closely. Margie studied his face, but he remained expressionless.

"Do you recognize her?" Margie asked softly.

"No, can't say that I do," Jeff said, handing the phone to her. "I think I'm going to head back to the party now."

"Jeff – Morgan is your daughter. Years ago, Kelly – she showed up at the house, all drenched in the rain, and –"

"Margaret, I didn't know that you set up this party as some sort of elaborate trap."

She took a step back. "It's not a trap, and at the time I didn't even know that Morgan was your daughter."

He laughed. "This is ridiculous, I have three kids. With you. Why are you doing this?"

Margie cleared her throat. She knew that tone, but she didn't fall for it anymore. He couldn't make her second guess herself.

"Jeff, please don't. I know the truth. Morgan has a picture of you and Kelly – more than one picture, actually."

He crossed his arms and stared at her for a moment.

After what felt like an eternity, he spoke. "What does it matter? Do you want me to take this girl under my wing or something now that her mom is dead?"

Margie sighed. "Jeff, this isn't a joke, this is real. Morgan is real. She's a lovely girl, and –"

"No." He said pointing a finger at her. "No, you don't get to do this. We're not even married anymore, why should I have to answer to you?"

"It's not that – it's not about answering to me, this girl is your flesh and blood. She's a half-sister to Connor and Jade and Tiffany. I thought it would be..."

Jeff scoffed. "You thought what? That I'd be happy about this? Happy that you dug up a ghost from twenty years ago?"

"She's not a ghost, she's a real person. And she's your *daughter.*"

He stared at her but didn't say anything.

"Don't tell me that you knew about this." Margie's voice rose. She couldn't stop it. "All this time, I thought that you *must* not have known, that Kelly didn't tell you, that she was too ashamed after she came to our home and saw that you were married."

"I need to rejoin the party."

He turned and walked back up the hill to the barn. Margie tried to take a deep breath, but it caught in her throat.

No – don't cry. Your makeup will run, and everyone will know you were crying. She looked out onto the ocean, trying to focus on the dark water glistening in the moonlight.

How was this possible? How could he be so callous? He wasn't surprised at all, it was like...he knew. He knew, and he didn't care.

He didn't *care*!

Margie had no illusions about Jeff, or at least she thought that she didn't. She always thought that deep down, under the mood swings and the critical comments, that he was a good man. A good person. Maybe a little rough around the edges, but...

A sob escaped from Margie's mouth. She hardly recognized it as her own voice. Her hand darted to her face. How could she have been so wrong about the man that she married? How could she have been such a fool?

She took a deep breath and collected herself before walking back up to the barn. As soon as this party was over, she needed to figure out what to tell Morgan. The kids needed to know the truth, too – the entire truth. That Kelly was right for all these years to not tell Morgan about Jeff. That Jeff was not a man worth knowing.

Margie went to the back of the barn and slipped into the bathroom. Her hair looked fine, but her makeup was running a bit. She was able to fix it well enough with her fingertips and was about to leave the bathroom when she heard Jeff's voice booming over speakers.

"Thank you all so much for coming out, it means the world to me. This is the best birthday party that I have ever had."

The crowd applauded. Margie stood inside the bathroom, gritting her teeth. She couldn't stand to go out and look at his face.

"I'd like to thank my beautiful girlfriend Tammy for organizing this party, and of course my lovely ex-wife Margie, and our three beautiful children. How about a round of applause?"

The partygoers obliged. Margie pulled the door open. How *dare* he use their children as some sort of trophy in front of his business friends? Was that all they ever were to him? A cover story to make him look like a decent guy?

Margie walked to the edge of the main dance floor. She didn't care that she was glaring at him in front of everyone. She didn't care what these people thought. All that mattered was that her kids knew the truth, and Margie was going to tell them everything.

Just as he finished his speech, Jeff went to hand off the microphone to Brandon, but someone else stepped in and took it. Margie couldn't quite make out who it was until the crowd dispersed. She gasped.

It was Morgan.

Chapter 21

He didn't even look at her face before handing off the microphone. He was already busy with shaking hands and taking pats on the back.

Morgan forced herself to smile. She knew that her face could look mean when she was angry – but she felt like she had a pretty good funnel for her anger at the moment.

She cleared her throat. "That was a beautiful speech, can we get another round of applause?"

The party guests politely clapped and Jeff took a mock bow. He turned to mouth a falsely humble "thank you" to Morgan when they locked eyes. She winked at him and watched as the smile faded from his face.

He recognized her. Good.

"I am *so* thankful that you could all make it here today. I know that I'm glad I could." She spotted Margie at the back of the barn, wide-eyed.

She continued. "Many of you may not know me, so I feel like I should introduce myself. My name is Morgan. I am twenty-two years old and twenty-three years ago, Jeff had an affair with my mother, Kelly Allen, and brought me into this world."

There were a couple of nervous laughs, but everyone stood still. Except for Jeff – he was headed straight for her.

In one swift movement, she hopped onto a table, sending some dishes shattering to the floor.

"Now the Cliftons certainly don't want you to know about me, because it *really* ruins the image of Jeff being a wonderful guy with a great family, complete with three beautiful children – not three and a half."

"Morgan, give me the microphone," Jeff said in a low voice. He was now standing at the table, arm outstretched, a stiff smile frozen on his face.

"What was that Jeff? You don't want all of these people to know that you're a cheater and a child abandoner?" She turned around and made eye contact with Margie. "What about you Margie? Inviting me into your home, pretending to care about me and my dead mom just so you could control the situation? Do you not want people to know that either?"

Margie shook her head but said nothing. She seemed frozen.

"And you Jade, where are you?" Morgan squinted, looking around the room. Jade was standing by the DJ booth, mouth hanging open.

"I *really* thought that we were close. I almost felt like you were a sister – before I even knew you were! But even *you* didn't want me around. Could having me in the family really be worse than your rude, controlling, loser DJ of a husband?"

Jeff had his hands clamped around her ankle now – and he was slowly pulling her leg. She tried to kick him away, but he was quite strong.

"I'm sorry, do you want me to get down or something?"

"Stop this or I will call the police," he said through gnashed teeth.

"You want to call the police on me Dad? Please do. Chief Hank almost arrested me once before, I'm not really worried about it."

There was a lot of murmuring in the crowd now, and Brandon was also at the base of the table, grabbing at her. Apparently, insulting his in-laws was okay, but insulting him was too much.

He was not as gentle as Jeff and leapt to snatch the microphone from her hand. Morgan raised it above her head so neither of them could reach it, but she realized that her time was limited.

"Is this your microphone DJ Brand?"

"Yeah," he grumbled. "Give it back."

Morgan leaned down as though she were going to hand it to him, but at the last second, she chucked it across the barn. There were gasps from the crowd, and the horrible noise it made when it landed gave her a chance to jump off the table and sprint back to her car.

She got there quickly and then fumbled with the keys to open the door – why did she even lock the car in the first place? It wasn't like she planned to stay long. She was just about to open the door when someone grabbed her shoulder and spun her around.

"*What* do you think you're doing?" said Jeff, and a bit of spit sailed from his mouth and onto her forehead.

She pulled away. "What's wrong? You don't want all your friends to know that you abandoned one of your children? Is that not the look you were going for?"

"You're going to pay for this," he said. "When I get my –"

"Stop it!" Margie's voice rang out behind them.

Jeff spun around to look at her, but he didn't release his hold on Morgan. For the first time, Morgan felt frightened – Jeff wasn't a big guy, but he was aggressive. Her shoulder throbbed underneath his grip.

Margie walked up to him and pried his arm away. "Take your hands off of her."

"Did you plan this entire party just so you could ambush me?" He was now leaning into her face, talking in a low growl. "You've *always* wanted to sabotage my business, but I never thought you'd go this far." He jabbed a finger into Morgan's chest.

"Ow!"

Margie grabbed his hand and ripped it away. "If you lay *one finger* on that girl again, I swear on my mother's grave that I will make you pay."

He laughed. "Oh yeah? What're you going to do? Do you think that I'm joking? You've done irreparable harm to my reputation and –"

"No Jeffrey. I think that *you* must be joking. The only one who's hurt your reputation is you. I've done nothing but support you for your entire life. And finally, I realize what a fool I've been. You are a bitter, greedy, and cruel little man, and you always have been. I am sorry that I ever helped anyone think differently of you."

"You're a real piece of work," he said. "I never thought your nastiness would come to this. What is it? Jealous of Tammy?"

They stared at each other for a moment, and Morgan took the chance to hop into her car, pull the door shut, and start the engine. She didn't need to be involved in their weird post marital problems.

She had problems of her own, including the fact that she told her dad that she was just going to get something she'd forgotten at Margie's place – and if she took much longer, he was going to be suspicious.

Morgan reversed down the driveway. At least she would never have to see any of their stupid faces again.

Chapter 22

Morgan took off and Margie turned to rush towards her car. She couldn't lose sight of Morgan – she needed to explain. But Margie was stopped when a hand grasped her wrist.

"Let me go Jeff," she said. Why was he so handsy all of a sudden?

"No. You need to go back in there and explain to everyone –"

Margie used her other hand to grab her fist and pull, breaking out of Jeff's hold. She learned that in a self defense class and felt a momentary joy that it worked.

"No Jeff. There's nothing to explain. Everything that she said about you was true. I'm not going to protect you anymore. I'm done making excuses for you. You're not a nice person. I don't know why it was so hard for me to admit. So guess what?"

He rolled his eyes. "What?"

"*You* get to explain this one!"

His face contorted into an angry scowl. Margie smiled to herself before turning to get into her car. She didn't know where Morgan was staying, but she had to find her – they couldn't end things like this. Morgan was angry, and understandably so – but she deserved to know the truth. The whole truth.

Margie got into her car and zipped down the driveway, but Morgan was nowhere to be seen. She knew that they were staying in Friday Harbor, so Margie turned left, guessing that Morgan must've gone that way.

Margie didn't like speeding, but this was an emergency. It paid off – in just a bit, Margie caught up to Morgan's bright white rental car.

She followed Morgan all the way into town and sat in her car and watched as she disappeared into a little house on the top of a hill. Luckily Margie was able to find street parking nearby and ran up to the front door, knocking forcefully.

There was no answer, but she could hear voices inside. She sighed and knocked again.

Clearly Morgan was trying to convince her dad not to check who was pounding like a crazy person, but it didn't work. A moment later, he opened the door.

"Can I help you?"

"Hi, are you Mr. Allen?"

"Yes. Do I –"

Margie stuck out her hand. "It's very nice to meet you, I'm Margie. Morgan has been staying with me for the past several weeks."

"Oh! It's so nice to meet you. I'm Ronnie Allen."

"Don't let her in Dad!" called Morgan's voice.

He gave Margie a puzzled look. "Is something going on?"

"Yes, there's been a big misunderstanding. Well – partial misunderstanding. I'm Margie Clifton – Jeff Clifton's ex-wife."

It took a moment before the recognition settled in on Ronnie's face. "*Oh*. Oh!"

He looked back into the house then back at Margie. "I don't know that I can..."

"Please, just let me come in and explain. To both of you. And I promise that I will never bother you again."

He shrugged. "Alright, come on in."

Margie took a deep breath and walked into the house. Morgan was nowhere to be seen.

"Please, have a seat," Ronnie said, motioning to the couch.

"Thank you." Margie sat down and looked around. "It really would be better if Morgan were here too. Do you think that you could convince her to hear me out?"

Ronnie smiled. "I can try."

He returned after only a few minutes, Morgan silently following behind him. Ronnie took a seat across from Margie, but Morgan remained standing, arms crossed.

"Well first off, I want to thank you both for giving me a chance to explain," said Margie. "I promise that I'll make it quick."

Ronnie's eyes darted between Morgan and Margie. "Okay. I'm all ears."

Margie smiled and began. "A few months ago, my brother invited me to San Juan Island as a surprise, and he sold me his property – the house and the barn and everything. For a dollar. And, long story short, it was because I really wanted a place to reunite my family. I mean – I guess I wanted to make a place that they could call home."

Morgan scoffed.

"I know," said Margie. "I know how that sounds. But you have to believe me – Morgan, I didn't know anything about you. Well...sort of."

Margie searched for her purse but realized that in her haste, she hadn't brought it with her.

"I was going to show you something, but I forgot all of my stuff. I keep a newspaper clipping of your mom with me at all times. When I was on the ferry, I saw the story about your mom passing away. And all of a sudden, it came back to me. Twenty-three years ago, your mom showed up at my house."

"So you *did* know," snapped Morgan.

Margie sighed. "Kind of. She was all – disheveled. And so was I, really. Connor was just born, and Jeff was away on business, as always. I invited her in, and she told me that Jeff was the father of her baby. And then she just ran off!"

"Yeah right," said Morgan. "My mom would never do something like that."

Ronnie cleared his throat. "It's true Morgan. Your mom – she didn't know, of course, that Jeff was married. When she met Margie – when she showed up at the house that night – it was just after she found out."

Margie's hand darted over her mouth. Poor Kelly – she was just a young girl then. How shocking it must've been for her – no wonder she behaved as she did.

"I never saw her or heard from her again," Margie said. "I had no idea what happened. I didn't even know her full name."

Margie paused before looking to Ronnie. "Did Kelly ever tell you if she reached out to Jeff?"

Ronnie nodded. "Yes, she did. He completely stopped responding to her – her calls, visits, letters. He acted like she never existed."

Margie's heart fell. She believed it – perhaps twenty years too late, but she knew it was true.

"So Mom just let him do that? She just – gave up?" asked Morgan.

"It wasn't really like that," said Ronnie. "You have to understand – your mom always had her pride. She didn't want anything from Jeff. She went back to her parents, and they promised to help her, and she finished school. And that's when we met. That's when I met you, and I fell in love with *both* of you. I never wanted you to have to know another father, especially one like him."

Morgan stared at him, eyes filled with tears. "But he didn't want me."

"He didn't know what he was missing," Ronnie stretched out, clasping Morgan's hands in his. "You are the best daughter that I could ever hope for. And you know that I can't have kids –"

Morgan groaned. "I know Dad."

"But you've always been my daughter. I love you. You always *will* be my daughter."

"I know," Morgan said, her voice softening.

Tears welled up in Margie's eyes. "I'm so sorry Morgan. I didn't even know until recently that you were actually Jeff's daughter – I *promise* that I was going to tell you everything. I wanted to talk to Jeff first, because I was sure that Jeff could not have possibly known you were born. I thought that if I told him, he'd be shocked and that he might..."

Morgan stared. "He might what?"

Margie sighed. "That he might behave like a decent human being. But he isn't a decent human being."

"Don't act like you were going to tell me all along. I know what you were doing."

Margie cocked her head to the side. "No sweetie, I didn't have a plan – that was the problem. I didn't know what to do. It wasn't until I accidentally found a picture of Jeff in your things that I knew the truth. And then I tried to call Jeff, but he wouldn't answer, and then –"

Morgan scoffed. "Brandon told me everything!"

"Brandon?" Margie shook her head slowly. "No. Of course. He overheard me on the phone – I was telling my sister after I realized that Jeff was your father. I called her because I didn't know what to do, and Brandon was sleeping in the other room, but I didn't know it –"

"Yeah, and he heard your whole plan."

"What plan? My plan was to talk to Jeff and see – well no, to tell him about you. Because I was convinced that he must not have known. But Morgan, I *promise* you, no one else knew. Jade didn't know, Tiffany didn't, Connor definitely didn't know – I was trying to figure out what to do. I wanted to have a family meeting to welcome you. I thought that Saltwater Cove could be a second home to you, too."

"You're lying," replied Morgan. "Brandon said –"

"Brandon is a spiteful idiot," said Margie.

Morgan's eyes widened. "Wow. I've never heard you say anything like that before."

"Well it's true," Margie said with a huff. "He's an angry, bitter little man, just like Jeff. I don't know what he told you, but I can promise you that he was doing it for his own gain."

Morgan bit her lip. "He told me that...well, he told me that you didn't want me to ruin the image of your perfect family, and you planned to run me off. And everyone was in on it."

Margie's jaw dropped. "He did not! Morgan, you have to believe me, that was completely untrue."

Ronnie chimed in. "You know honey, that doesn't really make a lot of sense. Why would she welcome you into her home, let you live there rent free all summer, cook for you, and generally be very welcoming?"

"I don't know," Morgan replied.

"I'm so, so sorry." Margie took a deep breath. "But I promise you, I didn't want to run you out of the family. I wanted to welcome you *into* it."

Morgan looked between her dad and Margie before bursting into tears. They both got up to hug her.

"I'm so sorry that I ruined the party," said Morgan. "Brandon got me all worked up, and like an *idiot* I took the bait and just –"

"It's okay, it's really okay," said Margie, patting her on the back. "The only thing that was ruined was Jeff's night. And he *more* than deserved it."

Ronnie pulled away. "What exactly did you do, Morgan?"

"Uh – it all happened so fast, I got ahold of the microphone and..."

Margie laughed. "It was quite a speech."

"I'm really sorry about those dishes," Morgan said.

"Morgan! I let you leave the house for half an hour!" exclaimed Ronnie. "I know you're a hot head, but this is too much!"

Margie waved a hand. "It's completely fine. A few dishes lost and a night to remember."

"Yeah, definitely one for the books."

Ronnie took a deep breath, but clearly decided he wasn't going to press for more information.

"Oh goodness!" Margie said when she saw the clock. "Look at the time. I need to get back to the barn and see what's going on. And I want you to pick a time to sit down with your new siblings. So we can clear everything up."

Morgan rubbed the back of her neck. "I don't know that I can face Jade ever again."

"Let me worry about that. I'm going to run now, but I will talk to you soon, okay?"

Morgan reached out and hugged her one more time. "Okay. And I'm really sorry, again."

"I'm sorry, too. About everything. But don't worry," Margie said, patting her on the back. "Families always have their little fights. I will see you soon."

Chapter 23

It was a busy and taxing day. Hank felt exhausted; when he picked Morgan up that morning, she was not in the best of moods. She was unusually quiet, which meant Hank had to talk more than he wanted to, but she didn't seem to be paying attention to anything that he said.

They were between calls at one point when she finally spoke. "I'm going to tell you something and you're going to get mad at me."

"Oh, I don't like the sound of that. What is it?"

"I went to a bunch of homes and businesses near the site of my mom's accident. And a lot of people had cameras that they said might have footage from the night my mom was hit."

"Okay...and did you find anything?"

Morgan sighed. "No, because no one got back to me with anything. But I was thinking that maybe you could help with that."

Hank laughed. "I can certainly ask nicely. If they have anything, I can take it into evidence."

"Good." Morgan crossed her arms. "I like the sound of that."

They spent about two hours in between calls checking in on those homes and businesses. Hank knew a lot of the people and was able to keep it friendly; he asked Morgan to stay in the car so that her grumpy face wouldn't scare people.

Hank felt bad – terrible, really – that they hadn't made much progress on the case, so he wasn't angry at her for trying to find things out on her own. But he was glad that she told him so that he could step in and actually handle the evidence. If they did find something, Morgan couldn't follow-up on it by herself. She would just end up in trouble again like she did with Brock.

By the end of their ride along, Morgan was a bit less icy to him, but not by much. He promised to follow up with her whether he heard anything or not. She thanked him and he dropped her off at the ferry terminal to wait for her dad.

It wasn't until 9 o'clock that Hank was finally able to take a seat on the couch and settle in front of the TV. He was ten minutes into an episode of *Parks and Recreation* when his phone rang.

It was Margie!

"Hello?"

"Is this Chief Hank?"

That definitely *wasn't* Margie. "Yes, who is this?"

"Hi Chief, it's Jade. Sorry to call you so late, but I was wondering if you knew where my mom was?"

Hank sat up. "I don't, is everything okay?"

"Oh – okay. Yeah, nothing is – well, I don't know. I don't think she's hurt or anything. I just thought she might be with you. She left her phone here, and Tiffany and Connor and I are leaving. I just wanted to let her know."

"Leaving where? What's going on?"

"It's a long story but...I have to go. Thanks Chief."

The line went dead. What on earth was going on? Where could Margie have gone that no one knew where she was? Shouldn't she be at the party?

Oh boy. Hank got a sinking feeling in his stomach. Maybe he didn't do a good enough job with keeping Morgan away from the party. He dropped her off at the ferry terminal just like he was supposed to, and the plan was that she was going to stay with her dad in that rental on Spring Street.

Hank jumped up and grabbed his car keys – he needed to find Margie in case something was wrong. He decided to head to Morgan's rental and see if she knew anything.

It was an agonizing fifteen minute drive to Friday Harbor. There wasn't much traffic on the road, but it felt like it was taking forever. He finally got to the house and knocked on the front door. It opened right away.

"Oh, hi Chief. You're not here to arrest me again, are you?" asked Morgan.

"That depends, what did you do this time?"

A smile brightened her face. "Nothing! What's up? Do you want to come in?"

"I was just looking for Margie actually, I didn't know if you knew where she was. Jade called me looking for her."

"Oh yeah. She was just here, but she left not too long ago. She was going back home – well, and to see what was going on at the barn."

"Did something happen? Is she okay?"

"Yeah, you could say something happened…" said Morgan. "But I'll let Margie tell you about it. No one is hurt or anything."

"Oh. Okay. I guess I'll stop by her place."

"Okay, have a good night!"

Well – at least *she* was back to her sunny self.

He needed to talk to Margie; he wanted to know what was going on, and he had to tell her how he felt. He couldn't take it any more.

Was it possible that he passed her on the drive over and didn't even notice? Hank got into his car and started the ride back to the other side of the island. He felt like he was chasing his tail, but now that he couldn't find Margie easily, it only motivated him more.

He got to Margie's place quickly. He checked the barn at first – there were a few people in there chatting, but no music or anything. Odd. Margie was nowhere to be seen, so he headed over to the house and knocked on the door.

After a moment, Margie answered. "Hank! What's going on, is everything okay?"

"Everything's fine, I want to make sure that everything was okay with *you*. I got a call from your cell phone – but it was Jade."

Margie sighed. "Oh."

"She didn't know where you were, and she said that they were all leaving? What's going on?"

"You'd better come inside."

He followed her in and saw that she was holding a piece of paper in her hands.

"What's that?"

She handed it to him. "It's a note from Jade. The kids were supposed to stay for the rest of the week. They were supposed to enjoy the house and the island and have some family time together but..."

"But what? What happened?"

"They're all leaving." Margie's voice broke. "They're catching the last ferry of the night and they're leaving. And it's all my fault."

"What? What could you have possibly done?"

Margie sighed. "It's a long story. And...I don't know if you'll ever want to look at me again after you hear the whole thing."

Hank looked at his watch – it was 9:40. The last ferry left Friday Harbor at 10 o'clock.

"How about you give me the one line version and we go from there?"

"One line version. Okay." She bit her lip. "Well – about a week ago, I found out that Morgan is my ex-husband's daughter. From an affair. From over twenty years ago, with Kelly Allen. And I didn't tell anyone because I was trying to...well, figure it out, and tell everyone in the right way, and I ruined everything."

Hank felt his jaw drop. "Wait, what?"

Margie covered her eyes with her hand. "I know...I didn't exactly know for sure, but I did suspect that it might be the case, but I didn't have proof, and –"

"It's okay," said Hank. "I believe you. I don't believe that you have a malicious bone in your body."

Margie laughed. "You're very sweet. But I lied to them – all of them. Morgan, Jade, Tiffany, Connor. I wanted a place that we could all be a family again – and instead, I pushed everyone away."

Hank felt his chest tighten. He knew exactly how she felt, because he too felt like his family fell apart after his wife passed away. He felt like he was struggling with everything in life, actually.

At least Margie was trying. And this business with Morgan...well, she could tell him the full story later. He believed down to his bones that Margie would never have hurt Morgan, or anyone for that matter, on purpose.

"Hey – listen. You've done something amazing here. You made Mike's rundown property something beautiful. This is going to be home for all of you, I know it. But we're running out of time here – the ferry will leave soon. Let me help."

"I don't know what can even be done. I've broken everyone's trust, I've hidden things, I've..."

Hank shook his head. "No, don't go down that path. Listen – do you have a picture of the kids?"

"Yes. I have one of the three of them from the party actually."

Margie opened up the gallery on her phone and scrolled through dozens of pictures of her children. Hank suppressed a smile – how could anyone accuse her of not being a dedicated mother?

"What do you need a picture for?"

"Can you text me one with all of them in it? I'm going to help you put your family back together."

She looked at him with surprise, but did what he asked. The picture popped up on his phone.

"You can tell me the rest of the story later. But please, don't feel so bad – I think you're doing great."

Margie's eyes brimmed with tears. "It doesn't feel that way."

"Hang tight, okay?"

She nodded. She looked so sad standing there that he couldn't help himself – he leaned forward and hugged her tightly before turning to walk out the door.

"You look beautiful by the way! I'll call you in a bit."

A smile dashed across her face for just a moment. "Okay!"

Hank rushed out to his car and made a phone call to the Sheriff's office. Luckily a buddy of his picked up – Deputy Howard.

"Hey – I got a favor to ask. This one is going to be off the books. I'm sending you a picture and I need you to apprehend these three before they board the ferry."

"Alright boss, I got you. I'm guessing you don't have an arrest warrant?"

Hank started the car. "Not exactly, but you can't let them leave the island."

"Alright. Are they dangerous?"

Hank laughed. "No. Not at all. Just some kids causing trouble."

"Is that what I tell them?"

"No." Hank paused. "Tell them they're in trouble for disturbing the peace. I'll be there in twenty minutes."

Chapter 24

"You can have a seat right in here."

Tiffany crossed her arms. "I'm calling my lawyer."

The deputy shrugged. "Okay. Might take him a while to get to the island." He shut the door behind him.

"I can't believe this. Who does he think he is?" Tiffany said.

"Do you really have a lawyer?" asked Connor.

She sighed. "Not exactly – but I have a *friend* who's a lawyer."

Jade stifled a giggle.

"Jade," Tiffany groaned, "how can you think this is funny?"

"I don't think it's funny, I'm just exhausted," Jade said, putting her hands up. "And I'm not the one who stumbled on the ferry and looked intoxicated in public."

"I'm not intoxicated!" replied Tiffany. "My shoes are really uncomfortable and my feet are killing me. I didn't expect that I would have to stand on that stupid trolley the whole way back."

"It doesn't make sense that he arrested all of us for *your* public intoxication offense," said Connor with a smile.

Tiffany rolled her eyes. "How can we be under arrest? Aren't they supposed to say the thing? You know – you have the right to remain silent, anything you say blah blah blah."

Connor turned to her. "Are you sure that *you're* not an attorney?"

Tiffany glared at him but said nothing. Jade sank into her seat. She didn't know what was going on, but she hated the thought of being in trouble with the law. She hated everything that happened that night, and she felt a bit delirious from it all.

Right after Morgan left, Brandon started a fight with her. He was offended by what Morgan said about him, and told Jade that if that's what her family thought of him, then he was never going to do another DJ event for them again.

Jade didn't know how to respond – no matter how many times she told him that Morgan was not speaking for her entire family, he just got angrier. He packed up all of his DJ equipment, got in the car, and left.

Meanwhile, their dad tried to smooth things over with his guests and told them that it was all a big misunderstanding; he said it stemmed from a girl who was grieving the death of her mother. He asked Jade to call the trolleys to take everyone back to town.

Jade did as she was told, but she felt like she was in a daze. She couldn't decide if she should go after Brandon and risk being the subject of his explosive anger, or go looking for her mom, or stay behind and try to keep everything together.

So instead of making a decision, Jade just stood in the barn. The guests cleared out, except for a few family members, and their dad pulled the three of them aside.

"If any of you say anything about this girl – this crazy girl – I am writing you out of my will. Do you understand?"

"Get over yourself Dad," Tiffany said. "Do you really think you can still control us with your money?"

Jade couldn't believe what she was hearing – surely there was a misunderstanding. "It's not true, is it Dad?"

"Of course not," he said instantly. "Clearly this con artist tricked her way into your mom's house."

"Whoa, really?" said Connor.

"Ha, yeah right." Tiffany scoffed. "I don't believe that for a second, and neither does anyone else."

"Tiffany," he replied in a low voice, "your ungratefulness has reached new heights today. Have some respect for your father."

She stared at him coolly for a moment before walking away. He immediately went after her, though Jade couldn't make out what he was saying, she could hear the anger in his voice.

A few of the guests didn't care much about the excitement and were still enjoying themselves – chatting, picking at dessert, admiring the barn. Jade looked for her mom, but couldn't find a sign of her anywhere. Her car was gone – but her purse was still in the house.

After not too long, the last trolley came to pick up the remaining guests. Almost everyone was gone, and Tiffany insisted that they get on the trolley.

"But shouldn't we wait for Mom?" asked Jade.

Tiffany shrugged. "I don't know Jade. I'm not waiting here. I'm not surprised that Dad acted like a scumbag, but if what that girl said was true – it seemed like Mom was in on it, too. I can't deal with this, I'm going home."

"I'm sure there must've been some misunderstanding," said Jade.

"Well, I'm not sticking around to find out," said Tiffany as she boarded the trolley.

Connor followed her, as he always did. Jade asked the trolley driver to wait for a minute so she could make a call to Chief Hank.

Unfortunately, he didn't know where their mom was either. Jade knew that she should probably go after Brandon anyway – so she decided to get on the ferry with her siblings.

Yet now, here they were, stuck in jail. Maybe for the rest of their lives!

The hysteria started to overtake her, all of the emotions flooding in. Jade felt tears pooling in her eyes. She was biting her lip, trying to hold it together, when she realized that the deputy hadn't searched her or taken away her cell phone.

Jade pulled out her phone and called Brandon.

"Yeah?"

He answered!

"Brandon! Thank goodness. Listen, we're in trouble, we're in the San Juan County Jail and I –"

"Sucks to be you then," he said. "I'm going home. Have a nice night."

The call disconnected.

Jade couldn't hold it in anymore – she started crying. It wasn't just Brandon, it was everything – everything that happened that night was overwhelming. There was so much anger and so many nasty words. Jade just wanted the night to be over.

Just then the door opened, and Chief Hank walked in.

"Chief Hank! It's *you*! Did you come to help us?"

"Hey Jade," he said slowly. "Yeah. You could say that."

Chapter 25

For almost an hour, Margie anxiously waited to hear from Hank. Finally, a call came through.

"Don't worry – everything is fine. Tiffany, Connor, and Jade are down here with me at the jail."

"Are they okay?"

"Of course. I had one of my deputies detain them so that we could – you know, talk."

Oh dear. "What did you talk about?"

"You know, this and that."

"Do they still want to leave?"

"They can't. The last ferry left for the night."

"Oh."

"Plus I told them that they can't leave."

Margie didn't know what to say.

"Are you still there?"

"Yes," she replied. "I'm still here. But I was hoping that they didn't leave because they wanted to talk to me."

"Of course they want to talk to you! anyway – who cares what they want. They're kids. Just come down here, tell them what happened, and tell them that they're going to stay here for a week and have some family fun, dang it."

Margie laughed. "It's not that simple."

"Eh, sure it is," Hank said. "I already talked to them for a bit. They know that everything you did was for them. Moving here, fixing up the house, fixing up that barn."

Margie felt a little flutter in her chest. "I don't think they'll believe that now."

"Of course they will. I mean – they do. I'm the Chief Deputy Sheriff, and I'm *pretty* sure they knew that I meant what I was saying."

Margie laughed again. Somehow he was able to make her feel better even though everything had gone so horribly wrong.

"Alright. I'll come down now."

Still in her pretty blue dress, Margie went out to the car and made the drive to Friday Harbor. The whole way there, she practiced what she was going to say and how she was going to say it. She anticipated some harsh questioning from Tiffany, and worried that perhaps Jade's trust was broken forever. Margie had no idea how Connor would react – he was always a wildcard.

Hank greeted her outside the jail and led her into the building. She opened the door, and as soon as she saw their three faces, promptly burst into tears.

All three of them jumped up to hug her, which caused her crying to intensify.

Finally she was able to get ahold of herself and sit down with them at the table. She told them the full story, with Jade interjecting only to clarify some details that she was present for.

When Margie finished, she remarked, "I can't believe you guys let me get that whole story out."

Connor laughed. "Yeah, the big scary police guy said that if we weren't nice to you that he'd open up some jail cells for us to spend the night in."

Tiffany rolled her eyes. "He was obviously joking. It was a very thinly veiled threat."

"I don't know if he was joking," said Jade.

"Well anyway," said Margie. "I didn't mean to hide anything from you kids. You are the most important people in my life. I just wanted to do things the right way and...I'm sorry."

"It's okay Mom. It all makes sense to me," said Jade.

Connor shrugged. "I mean it's weird, having a half-sister, but we'll get used to it. And I like Morgan's style."

"Yeah," Tiffany added. "I can't say that I *hated* her telling Dad off like that. I mean Mom – did you really think Dad was innocent in all of this?"

"Now you know that I don't like to say anything negative about your father –"

Tiffany cut her off. "Yeah, but sometimes you have to say the truth. Listen – I won't go there. I'm sorry that this party didn't go the way you'd hoped. And I'm sorry that Dad is self-ish. But he's always been that way. I'm over it – and, the thing is – what I *really* wanted to say is that I appreciate you trying to make this place nice for us. And I love you."

Margie felt tears coming to her eyes again. "Thanks sweetie. Does that mean that we can try doing this whole family week thing over again?"

"Of course Mom," said Jade.

She looked at them – they looked tired, but they were smiling. Margie took a deep breath. It didn't quite work out as she'd hoped – but it worked out in the end.

Now all that was left was to tell Hank the truth – and see if he could forgive her, too.

Chapter 26

It was only after they got out of jail and Jade got a good night's sleep that she realized they were never *actually* under arrest. In her tired and emotionally overtaxed state, she didn't question it. Clearly, it was Chief Hank's doing, and they likely could have left at any time.

She was glad they didn't leave, though. The next morning, they woke up and had breakfast together. It felt different – it felt like it used to be when they were kids. Before the divorce – and before they knew the truth about their dad.

Tiffany insisted that she wasn't surprised by the news at all, and Jade believed her; she was rather cynical and was historically the most harsh on their dad.

Jade, on the other hand, felt quite silly – like her mom, she'd always given him the benefit of the doubt. Now she didn't know what to think. He never apologized to them or attempted to explain anything. All he did was threaten to remove them from his will.

Who thought like that? It was disgusting to her; to think that she would sit around, waiting for him to die, so she could get some of his money. She had *no* interest in his money. All she ever wanted was her family to be happy again.

It seemed that they finally had that – they just had to remove their dad and add Morgan instead. It was a bit strange at first, but Morgan and her dad came to visit after the dust settled. She apologized to everyone individually; Jade, of course, accepted her apology without hesitation.

"I need to apologize to Brandon too," said Morgan. "I'm sorry about what I said."

"Well, he's been giving me the silent treatment," Jade told her. "But I can try calling him."

Morgan nodded. "Okay, that works. He was the one, after all, who told me the truth."

"Oh, that's right," said Jade. "I completely forgot that part of the story. What exactly did he say to you?"

"Well," Morgan said, biting a fingernail, "he said that you, Margie, your dad, and your siblings were trying to trick me into leaving town so I wouldn't ruin the image of your perfect family."

Jade's stomach dropped. "You're kidding."

"No," Morgan spoke quickly now. "I swear that's *exactly* what he said to me. And that's why I said all of those horrible things. Well no – I said all of those horrible things because I'm an idiot and I believed him. And I wanted to be really mean and get you guys back. But if I had stopped to think for a second, I would've realized that it couldn't possibly be true, and –"

"It's okay. I know that Brandon can be very...persuasive."

Jade saw her mom busying herself and fussing around them. "Mom, did you know about this? About Brandon?"

She stopped what she was doing. "I knew that he was the one who told Morgan about your dad, but I didn't know that he'd said all of *that*."

"I can't believe that he did that. Why would he do that?" asked Jade.

Her mom's eyes darted to Morgan, then back to her. Her facial expression remained neutral. "I'm not sure, honey. But it seems like something that you should talk to him about."

It took the rest of the night for Jade to digest that conversation. She was never a spontaneous person, and it took her a while to process new information. Yet it became clear that she *did* need to talk to Brandon; there was no excuse for what he said to Morgan.

Before breakfast the next morning, Jade went into her room and closed the door. She tried calling Brandon, but he didn't pick up. He was still ignoring her to teach her a lesson.

She knew why – he would tell her that she chose her family over him, just like he claimed she always did. But this visit with her mom and siblings was planned – she took time off of work so that they could all be together. He was invited too, of course. But he was angry, and he expected Jade to follow him. Normally, she would have. But this time...

An idea popped into her head – she sent him a text message saying that her company needed a DJ for an event that Friday. A minute later, her phone rang.

Bingo.

"Hello?"

"Alright Jade, give me the details of this job."

Oh dear – he was *not* being friendly. He was going to be livid when he found out that she made it all up. "I will. But first I need to talk to you."

"No. We're not doing this. Not while you're still over there. You need to come home."

Jade bit her lip. She needed to have this conversation with him. "I need to know why you told Morgan about my dad."

"What are you talking about?"

"I know that you were the one who told her the truth about my dad. Why didn't you tell me about it? I had no idea."

He scoffed. "Of course you had no idea, your family never tells you anything."

"I heard what you said to her. It was nasty. You made things up about me, and my mom, and –"

"I can't even believe you right now. You're being ungrateful."

She took a deep breath. "How am I being ungrateful? Why would I want you to be mean to Morgan? She's my half-sister."

"Oh boy, here we go. So she's your sister now? Another one? It's always about your *family*. You find a new half-sister and suddenly she's even more accepted that I am."

"Don't be like that Brandon. If you were here, spending time with everyone, you'd be accepted too, and –"

"No I wouldn't. You heard those things that she said about me – it's what all of your family thinks of me, isn't it? Meanwhile, I'm working my *butt* off to make something really special, and you *know* that I have talent and I'm one of the best DJs in the state!"

How did he always manage to make things about him being a DJ?

"Brandon, no one thinks those mean things about you. The only reason that Morgan said any of it was because you told her that everyone was trying to run her out of the family. And that *wasn't true*. Why would you say that?"

"For you, you *idiot*! What did you think was going to happen when Morgan found out that your dad was her dad?"

"Well, I thought that –"

"You didn't think, did you? You didn't realize that Morgan was going to go after her part of the inheritance. Why wouldn't she? She's just as much his kid as you are."

Jade's jaw dropped. "*What?*"

"Maybe in your world, where everything is a mystical la-la land and people are fair and kind –"

Jade cut him off. "You told her lies about us so that she wouldn't go after my dad's money? What is wrong with you?"

"What's wrong with *you*! You know that we need that money."

"How can money be all that you think about? How can that even – you're not even –"

"I'm not having this conversation with you right now. You're being way too emotional. Are you going to give me the contact information for that job or not?"

Jade didn't respond for a moment. Her head felt all jumbled. "Just forget about it."

She disconnected the call and sat there, listening to the laughter rising from the kitchen – it sounded like Connor was telling a story with his best British accent, for some reason.

Jade felt so strange sitting in that room, alone, the ceiling fan rotating slowly above her. She was so close to her family, yet still felt so far away.

She ran through her conversation with Brandon and tried to sort out what happened. Brandon said she was being emotional, and he called her an idiot. Normally, she brushed these sort of comments off; he said stuff like that all the time. But there was something that she couldn't shake – something that bothered her more than anything.

Jade stood up, her head still muddled, and went to look at her reflection in the mirror. Her cheeks were red and her chest looked splotchy – she couldn't go back into the kitchen looking like this. Her mom would instantly know that something was up.

But she felt so angry at Brandon for saying those horrible things to Morgan that she couldn't help it. Her skin got angry for her.

She took a deep breath and decided that she needed to calm down. It was a beautiful day, and she still couldn't believe how lovely everything was here – the house, the barn, and the incredible view.

"Brandon thought that Uncle Mike should have left all of this to him. He was mad about that too," she muttered to herself.

She sat back down on the bed. Brandon wasn't always diffi-cult – when they first started dating, he was like a model boyfriend. Jade couldn't believe how sweet and thoughtful he was; all of her friends were jealous. Not that Jade cared for that, but it made her feel like she'd gotten a wonderful partner. She didn't even think twice when he proposed.

It wasn't until they graduated school and he had a hard time finding work that he started to get the way he was now. Moody, obsessed with money. Obsessed with his talent. Self-centered.

Jade felt guilty because her job search was easy. So when Brandon came up with his DJ thing, she wanted to support him. She thought that maybe if he could follow his dreams, he would get back to being the nice guy that she knew.

But he'd been like this for years, and now it seemed that all he could think about was money. Especially money that didn't belong to him. Properties, inheritances – he was so much like...

Jade took a deep breath. It was hard to admit it to herself. But Brandon was *so much* like her father.

She was still sorting out how she felt about her dad after what he did to Morgan – but there was a voice in her head that kept repeating, "Do you really want to be married to someone like Dad?"

She got up and looked at herself in the mirror again. Her cheeks were almost back to normal, so she decided to rejoin her family and put these things out of her mind.

Back in the kitchen, she successfully hid that anything happened. She was grateful that Morgan didn't ask about

Brandon – though Morgan did give her a bit of a funny look when she relayed that they'd spoken for a bit.

After breakfast, Chief Hank took them all out on his boat. Jade left her phone at home, because after she hung up on Brandon, he didn't take it well. He started calling her repeatedly and sending her text message after text message.

They had a wonderful time out on the water, and it was a great distraction. Jade allowed things to settle in her mind. By the end of the day, she'd given her thoughts about Brandon enough room to breathe. She felt comfortable with them. She was no longer horrified that Brandon was so much like her dad – well, she was still disgusted by him, but she was no longer shocked.

When they got back from the boat, Jade quietly excused herself and went back to her room. She had sixteen missed calls and a whopping thirty-four text messages from Brandon.

It was interesting, in a way, to scroll through the messages and watch him cycle through different moods. At first he was pleading, then he was angry, then he berated her, and lastly he apologized before starting all over again.

She took a deep breath and called him. He picked up right away.

"Where have you been all day, I thought you were dead!"

"I'm not dead. I've taken the day to think."

"Okay? It took you all day to think?"

Jade cleared her throat. "Brandon, we are getting a divorce."

He was silent for a moment. "Excuse me?"

"We are going to get a divorce," she repeated. She kept her tone even – this wasn't going to be an argument.

"Are you kidding me? Just because I said something mean to your half-sister? I'm sorry, okay? I'm *really* sorry. I can't believe how much you're overreacting about this."

"I'm going to meet with an attorney early next week. We can talk more after that."

"You have got to be kidding –"

Jade disconnected the call and turned off her phone. She felt emotionally drained, but at the same time, there was a lightness in her chest. Her heart felt happy for the first time since she could remember.

She slipped her phone into her purse and went back to the living room, where everyone was trying to make S'mores in the fireplace.

Chapter 27

After a wonderful week together, it was finally time for Margie to say goodbye. Morgan was the first to go – she left early in the week with her dad. Margie made her promise that she would come and visit – and that she would finish her degree at school.

"I'm sure that's what your mom would've wanted," Margie said.

Morgan smiled. "I know. Thank you again – for everything."

"Always remember that you're welcome here. Anytime, okay? This is your home too."

A smile spread across Morgan's face. "Thanks Margie. That means a lot."

On Saturday, Margie drove the kids to the ferry terminal.

"Don't worry Mom," said Tiffany. "We'll be back soon. I'll try to organize the next visit."

"I'm in for anything," added Connor. "Just let me know when."

"Okay sweetie," Margie said, giving him a tight hug. "Safe travels! You have to let me know when you get home safely."

"We will," they all said at once.

"I think I'll come back next weekend," said Jade. "It seems I might have more free time on my hands in the future."

"That would be lovely," Margie replied.

She secretly hoped that Jade might move in with her during the divorce, but she decided not to bring it up for the time being. Jade was exceedingly private, and Margie knew that when the time was right, she would hear the full story.

Everyone was shocked, of course, when Jade announced that she planned to divorce Brandon. Margie was shocked, too – but also ecstatic. She never believed the day would come. As much as she hated for one of her kids to have to go through a divorce, it did seem that Brandon was beyond change. Jade already seemed happier and less weighed down.

When Margie got back home, she stood in the kitchen for a moment and absorbed the silence. It was strange. She wasn't used to being by herself – she was hardly moved in before Morgan appeared on her doorstep.

Now everyone was gone, and the house was silent, but her heart still felt full.

Everyone loved the house, they loved the island, and for the most part, they got along for the entire visit. Margie chuckled to herself – it was a lot to ask for an entire week. It seemed that getting all of their fighting out of the way at the party was the perfect way to start the vacation.

Margie still hadn't heard a word from Jeff, and she didn't expect to. He was probably still in damage control from the party. Margie's first instinct was to feel bad about what happened, but she dismissed that quickly. He brought it all on himself, and he deserved whatever people thought of him. He simply wasn't a nice guy; maybe he was, once, but that time passed. And it was freeing for Margie to finally be able to admit that.

She was busy cleaning up the house and washing the linens when her phone rang.

"Hello?"

"Hey Margie! It's Hank. How are you doing?"

"Well hi Hank! I'm doing pretty good, just putting things in order. How are you doing?"

"Good, really good. Did everyone safely get aboard the ferry?"

"Yes they did," she said with a laugh. "No arrests this time."

"Good, glad to hear it. I was wondering – well, I have a proposition. I feel like I've been very lucky to enjoy a lot of your lovely dinners, and I thought that maybe you might want to come over to my place tomorrow so I can cook for you?"

Margie smiled. That was certainly a change of pace. "Well – sure! That would be nice."

"I'm a bit rusty, but I think I can make you something good."

"I'm sure it'll be great. What time should I come over?"

"How about seven?"

"Perfect! And what can I bring?"

"Just your beautiful self," he said. "See you then."

Margie felt herself blush. "Okay, see you then."

As sweet as his little compliment was, she tried to ignore it and instead think of what to bring. She would never *dream* of showing up empty handed at a dinner party. She decided to make a strawberry shortcake for dessert, because who could complain about a bit of shortcake?

She spent an embarrassingly long time picking an outfit for the dinner. She didn't mean to – she just suddenly had a lot of free time. Of course Jeff never made dinner for her, so she was really interested to see what this would be like.

Plus, Margie finally had to tell Hank the full story about Morgan. She dreaded it, but it was time. He'd gotten part of the story, but who knew how he would feel when he heard the whole truth.

She felt a bit nervous as she drove to Hank's house the next evening. Hank was outside grilling when she pulled up to the house.

"Hey there!" he said with a wave.

"Hi," Margie said as she got out of the car. "What cha cooking there?"

"I've got grilled marinated vegetables, baked potatoes, and some steak."

Margie caught herself staring at him in his black apron. How could he make an apron look masculine? "It smells amazing."

"Thank you! It's a bit chilly, do you want to wait inside?"

Margie shook her head. "No, I'd like to see how you work here. Maybe you could teach me a few tricks – I'm not a skilled grill master by any means. I do have a dessert for later, though. Maybe I can put that inside?"

"What do we have here?" Hank said as he peered over. "It looks incredible."

"Thank you. It's a strawberry shortcake. And I brought some vanilla ice cream. I'll just go and set it inside."

Margie went into the kitchen and put the ice cream in the freezer, but left the strawberry shortcake out on the counter. On her way back outside, she caught sight of the dining room table – there was a white tablecloth, candles, and a dozen yellow roses. Her hand darted to her mouth – was this all for her? It seemed very...romantic.

Oh dear. It was time to set the record straight.

"Hank," she said when she got back outside, "it's time for you to hear the whole truth. I need to tell you everything about Morgan, from start to finish. And Jeff. I've been dreading telling you, because it doesn't put me in the best light. I was hiding things, and kind of lying to you – but I really want to –"

He held up a hand. "Can I tell you something first, and you promise not to get angry at me?"

Her get angry at *him?* Did he do something and not tell her – like arrest Jeff too?

"Oh – okay. Sure. What is it?"

He closed the lid of the grill. "Remember when you were at the jail and told your kids the whole story?"

"Yeah?"

He cleared his throat. "I was sort of, kind of, listening."

Margie suppressed a smile. "Oh?"

"I didn't mean to eavesdrop. I just wanted to make sure they gave you a chance to talk, and if they didn't, I was going to play bad cop and say something."

Margie started to laugh. "I think you had Jade pretty scared. And Connor – well, he was just confused. It worked, though; I got to tell them everything."

"I know! And I should've stopped listening, but..."

"You were just *riveted*?"

Hank laughed. "I was. I knew that you were really worried about telling me everything, and I kind of needed to know why."

"It's because I'm a liar!" Margie exclaimed. "And I tricked you into helping me with all this stuff and I never told you what was going on! And I feel awful about it, and I don't know if you can forgive that."

"A woman has to have her secrets." Hank shrugged. "I never felt like you were using me or anything – you never lied to me, you just withheld some information. Until it could be confirmed. Top notch investigative work, really."

"I guess you can look at it that way."

"But I guess," he said, stepping forward, "that I would have to ask you to not hide things from me in the future."

Margie nodded. "Of course not, and I won't do anything like that again. There are no other horrible secrets. That I know of!"

"No," Hank said, getting a little closer. "I mean – I don't want you to keep any secrets from me. Because I'd like to –

what I'm trying to say is, I want to be part of your life. In a, uh, romantic way."

Oh!

"Is that why there are candles on the table?" Margie asked.

Hank nodded. "Yes, that was really supposed to set the mood. I thought this conversation could happen over candle light, when you couldn't really see me very well, so it'd be easier to trick you."

"You don't have to trick me," replied Margie. "I very much like what I see."

He made a face that suggested she said something shocking before continuing. "The thing is, Margie, that I've been in a slump since Corinne passed away. And the day that you walked into the sheriff's office – everything changed. You woke me up, dusted me off. You brought light back into my life. You're an amazing woman, and to tell you the truth, I don't think that I can go another minute without you knowing that you are the first thing I think about when I wake up in the morning, and the last thing I think about when I fall asleep at night. I'm crazy about you."

Margie looked at him for a moment. He looked so handsome, and somehow this vulnerability in his eyes only added to his gruff mystique.

"You know how to make an old woman blush."

He leaned down so his face was close to hers. "There are no old women here. There is, however, a beautiful, vibrant, and addicting woman that I need to have in my life."

Margie felt the butterflies take off in her stomach – something that she never expected to feel again. She giggled. She felt like she was eighteen, giddy and silly. "You know Chief, you're not so bad yourself."

He leaned forward slightly and kissed her. She wrapped her arms around his neck and kissed him back.

In a moment, he picked her up.

"No!" She yelled through laughter. "Put me down! You're going to hurt your back!"

He was smiling broadly now. "I'm not just brave, you know. I'm strong too."

"Is that so?"

In a single motion, he literally swept her off her feet. Margie giggled like a schoolgirl as he carried her into the house and placed her into her seat at the table.

"Now Miss," he said briskly, lighting the candles, "if you have it in your big heart to accept a grumpy Chief into your life, then he'd like to serve you the first of many fabulous dinners."

"I thought you'd never ask."

Epilogue

Morgan stepped off of the ferry and into the cool October air. She stood for a moment, taking in the beautiful sight of the buildings in Friday Harbor. It'd been a few months since she'd been to the island, but her last visit was always in the back of her mind. Despite her wild outburst at the surprise party, she had the fondest memories of her time there – and she couldn't wait to come back.

Her phone rang; it was Jade. "Hello?"

"Hey girl. I can see you, can you see me?"

Morgan looked around but struggled to peer over the crowd. "Not yet – where are you?"

"I'm close enough to see you just standing there and sucking in all the air with a big smile on your face."

Morgan laughed. If it was anyone other than Jade, she would have felt embarrassed. But Jade was really starting to feel like her sister. She and Jade kept in almost constant contact since the fateful birthday party; they had a lot to talk about – she went back to school for the semester and Jade focused on work and her divorce.

If someone told Morgan that first day that she stepped off of the ferry that she would have Jade, her half-sister, as one of her closest friends, and Margie, her absent father's ex-wife, as a sort of surrogate aunt – she would've told them that they were crazy.

But here she was, and her heart swelled with joy.

Morgan finally caught sight of Jade and hurried up the hill to meet her. "Sorry about making you wait. It's just – well, there's something about coming back here."

"I hope it's a good something," said Jade as she loaded Morgan's suitcase in the car.

"It's definitely a good something."

Jade kept her up to date with all of the happenings on San Juan Island. Fortunately, there wasn't much excitement since she'd left. Chief Hank and Margie were dating, and it seemed that Margie had never been happier; also, the barn really took off as an event space, which Margie totally deserved.

In contrast, Jade continued through the slog of her divorce, though she never really complained about it.

"What's the update on Brandon?" Morgan asked.

Jade sighed. "Well, I'm still paying for his attorney."

"Right."

"And that attorney is now trying to argue that Brandon needs spousal support."

"Oh boy. Is he ever going to stop being a weasel?"

"Who knows," Jade said airily. "Will you need to change or anything before we go out?"

Morgan shook her head. "No, the trip wasn't too bad."

When they got to Margie's place, everyone was already inside – Connor, Tiffany, and of course Chief Hank. The house smelled wonderful – Margie made a bunch of fall treats to throw a sort of welcoming party. There were sweet potato tater tots, sangria with cinnamon sticks that smelled *amazing*, soft pretzels with cheese, butternut squash pizza, and of course, pumpkin pie.

She said hello to everyone, and to her surprise, there were hugs all around – even from Tiffany. Tiffany was much more reserved than her other siblings, but it seemed that she was certainly trying to be welcoming.

"There's my favorite 'hiker,' " Chief Hank said with a smile.

"Chief!" Morgan offered a salute. "I'm reporting for duty. I'm here to help you arrest this family if they get out of hand."

"I may be taking you up on that," he replied.

"Morgan! I'm so happy you could make it!" Margie pulled her in for a hug and Morgan felt her body relax.

She couldn't put her finger on exactly what Margie smelled like – but it was some sort of mix of lavender and lemongrass. Both of those smells now had such a calming effect on her.

"Thanks so much for having me, it's wonderful to be back."

"Well! Eat up, we need to get going in a bit or we're going to miss the documentary!"

After a bit more chatting and snacking, they split into two cars and made their way into town. Tiffany organized this family get together, and for some reason, she chose the Friday Harbor Film Festival.

"Is Tiffany really into movies or something?" asked Morgan as they made the drive over.

"She is," said Jade. "If you can believe it, she has quite the artistic side."

Morgan thought on that for a moment. "Yeah, I can see that. I can definitely see that."

They missed the films that were shown early in the morning, but there were documentaries all weekend, along with events. They were able to get seats at the Whittier Theatre for the evening to enjoy one of the feature-length documentaries on the challenges that the Southern Resident Killer Whales faced.

Despite looking forward to this event for weeks, Morgan felt herself growing shy now that she was back with the Clifton family. Did they really want her there? Was Tiffany just being nice, or did she actually forgive her for her craziness that past summer?

Morgan retreated into herself and stayed quiet, and enjoyed listening to their joking and teasing; everyone was having fun together again. Morgan was having fun, too, but she forgot how much of an intruder she felt like when she was with them all – part of her wanted to jump back on the ferry and run away.

The film started not too long after their arrival, and it was wonderful – there were beautiful videos of the killer whales shot around the San Juan Islands and also along the coast where they chased their Chinook salmon meals.

After it was done, everyone was abuzz with excitement and opinions on what should be done to protect the whales.

Morgan found herself listening and laughing along, but offered no opinions of her own.

They mingled with people in the lobby of the theater for a while; it seemed like Hank was the mayor or something. Everyone knew him, and Margie wasn't much different. After a short while, Margie insisted that they get back home.

The plan was for a small after party at Saltwater Cove. Margie volunteered the barn, of course – though most weekends were booked with weddings and events, Margie made an exception to save this night for the film festival, and she wanted everything to be perfect.

When they got back to Saltwater Cove, Margie ran off to prepare a few last minute things, and Chief pulled them all aside.

"Alright kids, I've got some good news and some bad news. What would you like first?"

"Hm," said Tiffany. "The good news?"

"Okay." He reached into a bag and handed them each a candle. "The good news is I got all of you a candle."

They looked at each other, puzzled.

"What's the bad news?" asked Connor. "Are you going to have us catch a rival barn on fire?"

Jade snorted a laugh.

Chief maintained his serious scowl and kept talking. "No, but I like where your head's at. The bad news is that I'm going to do something that will embarrass Margie a whole lot today. I'm going to propose to her – with your permission, of course."

Morgan quickly looked between the siblings to see how they reacted to the news.

Jade spoke first. "That's amazing! She's going to be so happy."

"Shouldn't you be asking me for permission or something?" asked Connor.

Tiffany rolled her eyes. "Yes Connor, everyone should ask you for permission to do anything at any time."

He laughed. "I'm just kidding. That's great, as long as you're good to her. If not..."

"We'll lock *you* up in that jail," said Tiffany. "But it seems like you make Mom really happy. So...yeah, I'm cool with it."

"Me too," added Connor. "What took you so long dude?"

Morgan couldn't help it; she giggled. "Give him a break, it's only been a few months!"

Chief laughed and shook his head. "I know. But I'm crazy about her. And when you're old, you don't have time to wait."

That made everyone laugh.

"It really means a lot that you guys are happy about this," he said. "I think that I was more nervous to talk to you than to her. What do you think, Morgan?"

Morgan realized that she had taken a step back from the group. "Oh – I don't know. I'm just...I'm not part of the family."

Tiffany outstretched a hand. "Of course you are. Mom would never dream of leaving you out. And neither would we."

Morgan felt something catch in her throat. She cleared her throat and accepted her hand. "Thanks Tiffany. I know it's kind of weird, and –"

"It's not weird," Jade said. "You're part of the family now. Forever. And ever, until you die."

"Whether you like it or not," Connor added.

Morgan beamed. "I'd like that very much."

"Good," Tiffany said with a smile. "You're in. So where do you want us Chief?"

"Or should we start calling you...Dad?" asked Connor.

Everyone groaned and Tiffany poked him in the shoulder. "Can you stop joking around for like fifteen minutes?"

Smiling broadly, Connor nodded.

"Alright," Chief said, directing them to stand against the wall. "I'm going to lead her through this back door, and the lights will be off, except the candles."

They all got into place, and Morgan realized that there were flowers all around the caterer's kitchen. It was Chief's doing – he certainly had a touch.

"Oh man – I almost forgot. Morgan – I have some news. I got a video from that night your mom was hit."

"What? Are you serious?"

He nodded. "We don't know much. But we have a video of the car, I just got it yesterday."

"That's amazing!"

"Yeah. It was at the right time, it seems. But there's something strange."

"What?"

"A woman was driving the car."

"Who was she?"

"We don't know who it was yet. We're working on it. Sorry to drop this on you – I just didn't want to forget in the excitement."

Morgan nodded, her head spinning. "Okay."

"Go get Mom before she decides to whip up a last minute cake or something," Jade urged.

Chief nodded before disappearing out the back door. They stood there, lit only by candlelight, giggling and trying to keep quiet.

A few minutes later, they could hear Margie approaching.

"We don't *need* the kitchen today because the caterers are only doing hors d'oeuvres and they're going to bring them in so –"

"Surprise!" Connor shouted when she walked in the room.

Margie jumped back a bit. "Kids! What are you doing in here?"

They said nothing. Jade pointed for her to turn around.

Puzzled, Margie slowly spun around and saw Chief Hank down on one knee. She gasped.

"Margie Clifton, I've brought you here today not to scare the crap out of you, but to ask you a question."

"No!"

"No?" he said.

"I mean – no, I mean, I can't –"

"Let the man talk, Mom," Tiffany said, laughing. Morgan started laughing too, and soon no one could resist.

Chief Hank stood up, hands on his hips. "Pull it together people, I'm trying to propose to this wonderful woman here."

"I didn't mean no!" Margie said.

"Oh good, I thought that was kind of a fast answer." He got back down on one knee and they tried to suppress their giggles. "Margie Clifton, you are an amazing woman and the sunshine of my life. Please ignore these hecklers when deciding...will you marry me?"

"Yes!" she squealed, jumping up and down. "What I meant to say was *yes, you lovely man!*"

He got up and hugged her. Morgan, Jade and Tiffany all cheered "Yay!" and put their candles down so that they could clap.

Margie turned to hug them all. "Did you all know about this?!"

"Nah, we just found out like ten minutes ago," Connor said.

"But we're all happy for you," added Tiffany, shooting Connor a stern look.

She squeezed them tightly before letting go. "This is too much! I can't run a party now!"

"Yeah," Jade said. "We have to keep our wits about us so Morgan doesn't get on the microphone again."

Morgan groaned. "You guys weren't supposed to know what I was planning this time."

Margie darted from the front door of the kitchen, to the back door, and then back to the front door. "I'm not sure what to do next! I think I'm in shock! Hank! I can't believe you!"

"The ring is really pretty, Mom," commented Jade.

Margie looked down at her hand. "Oh my goodness, it is! I didn't even really see it! Hank!"

He shrugged. "What can I say, I had some help."

"From who?"

Tiffany slowly raised a hand. "Guilty."

"Tiffany!" Margie exclaimed. "And you didn't tell me he was going to propose?"

"I didn't want to ruin the surprise!"

"Well that's it," Margie said, pulling herself up to sit on the counter. "I'm done for the night. You guys are too much. All of you!"

"Hey," Morgan said with a smile. "How about when I graduate I come back and help you plan this big wedding."

"A wedding!" Margie said, fanning herself. "For an old woman like me! That is just –"

"Oh come on Mom, you have to do something. You have this great barn after all," said Jade.

Margie's cheeks were flushed red; she was clearly stunned, but couldn't stop smiling. "We can figure that out later."

"It'll be just like old times," said Morgan. "You and me driving U-hauls, but minus the impending doom."

Jade laughed. "That sounds pretty good."

"It does," Margie said, dabbing the corners of her eyes with a tissue. "It really does. I love you all *so* much. I honestly don't know what to do with myself."

Chief offered a hand to help her down from the counter. "Well how about, my beautiful bride, we take it one day at a time, and go and enjoy this lovely party you've set up?"

Margie accepted his hand and hopped down. "That's a wonderful idea."

Morgan waited for everyone else to leave the kitchen, and paused for a moment. She was happy for Margie and Hank. She felt warm all over, being welcomed into the family for a moment like that.

Even better, there was news in her mom's case. She'd be back to San Juan soon and there would be no shortage of excitement.

A glimmer of hope swelled in her heart. Morgan shut off the kitchen lights and jumped into a brief jog to catch up to her half-siblings.

Introduction to *Saltwater Studios*

The truth can set you free...or completely destroy you...

Morgan Allen has neither the time nor the patience for shenanigans. Running her wedding photography business by day and searching for new evidence in the cold-case death of her mother by night leaves no room in her life for much else. Too bad her infuriatingly charming videographer seems so intent on overwhelming her with shenanigans and forcing his way into her heart...

Luke Pierce has no idea why Morgan is so resistant to his charms. All he knows for sure is that he's willing to do anything to change her mind about him—even if it means going against the deeply ingrained instincts that normally cause him to run from anything too complicated or emotional. Something tells him Morgan's worth the effort...and the potential broken heart.

But just as Luke begins to win Morgan over—just as she begins to let him win her over—a dark secret surfaces, threatening to ruin everything they've built together. When all is said and done, will the truth Morgan's been searching for destroy her chance at happily ever after with Luke?

In book two of the Westcott Bay series, return to San Juan Island and get the full story of Margie's wedding planning, Jade's new digs and Morgan's shot at a happily ever after! Get your copy on Amazon today to start binge reading!

Would you like to join my reader group?

Sign up for my reader newsletter and get a free copy of my novella *Christmas at Saltwater Cove*. You can sign up by visiting: https://bit.ly/XmasSWC

About the Author

Amelia Addler writes always clean, always swoon-worthy romance stories and believes that everyone deserves their own happily ever after.

Her soulmate is a man who once spent five weeks driving her to work at 4AM after her car broke down (and he didn't complain, not even once). She is lucky enough to be married to that man and they live in Pittsburgh with their little yellow mutt. Visit her website at AmeliaAddler.com or drop her an email at amelia@AmeliaAddler.com.

Also by Amelia...

The Westcott Bay Series

Saltwater Cove

Saltwater Studios

Saltwater Secrets

Saltwater Crossing

Saltwater Falls

Saltwater Memories

Saltwater Promises

Christmas at Saltwater Cove

The Orcas Island Series

Sunset Cove

Sunset Secrets

Sunset Tides

Sunset Weddings

Sunset Serenade

The Billionaire Date Series

Nurse's Date with a Billionaire

Doctor's Date with a Billionaire

Veterinarian's Date with a Billionaire

Made in the USA
Monee, IL
15 November 2023

46593745R00142